END GAME

THE HARRY STARKE NOVELS BOOK 16

BLAIR HOWARD

DEDICATION

For Jo, as always

PROLOGUE

Thursday, July 12, 2019

Laredo, Texas

Early Morning

As he expected, the streets of Laredo were quiet. It was, after all, just after three in the morning. He took the ramp onto Interstate 35 South, making sure to keep within the speed limit.

The sky was dark, the summer air warm. As the highway rose and fell from one overpass to the next, he looked out over the hood of his car. In the distance, the US-Mexico border was only a couple minutes away, a border he'd crossed more times than he could count. If all went well tonight, within a couple of weeks he'd be far away, in Canada maybe, with enough money to live comfortably for the rest of his days. Maybe he'd learn to ski or something. Hunt a moose. Who the hell knew?

Over the next rise, he spotted the Denny's sign, nodded to himself and took the exit. A few minutes later, he pulled into the back parking lot that Denny's shared with the La Quinta Inn.

The Denny's was open 24 hours, though it was near empty when he walked inside. He was careful to open the door with his right hand, keeping his left in his pocket. It had to be his right hand.

He took a seat near the door and a waiter with strange-looking tattoos on his arm—Arabic, maybe—approached, a carafe of coffee in hand, and looked expectantly at him. The man glanced up at the waiter and nodded. The waiter poured, placed the carafe on the table and took out his order pad. The man ordered two eggs over easy, bacon and toast, knowing he wouldn't touch it.

In fact, he was careful not to touch anything at all, and he certainly couldn't eat or drink anything. One stray fingerprint or DNA sample, and the whole thing would be blown to bits... And El Coco wouldn't be happy about that, now would he?

He looked around the restaurant. An older woman, probably a night-worker at the motel, was seated at the counter with her back to him sipping coffee. Other than her and the Denny's staff, the place was empty. The TV —the sound turned off—was replaying yesterday's news. The Mexican president was speaking passionately from a podium, but the man had no idea what he was saying.

Tweets from President Trump were displayed to one side of the screen.

The man watched the TV with a passing interest. Politics had never interested him. He preferred things he could touch, changes in his life he could measure. Like the weight of the gun snug in a tuck-in holster at the small of his back. That was real, heavy, and lethal, more real to him than anything the TV could show at three o'clock in the morning.

The door opened and closed, and the man turned to see an older gentleman in jeans and a button-down shirt walk in. A holstered 1911 hung from his belt. He was wearing a white cowboy hat and tan western boots. Thick sideburns framed his leathery face. As the older gentleman sauntered by, the man looked up at him and nodded.

Right on time.

He watched the man in the white hat take a seat. He watched as he ordered something from the waiter with the tattoos.

Probably the same thing he ordered yesterday. The man was a Texas Ranger, and his habits were predictable, like clockwork.

The man smiled to himself and rose from his seat, happy that the Ranger hadn't taken any notice of him, and walked calmly toward him, as if he was heading toward the restrooms.

The Ranger didn't notice him approaching until it was too late. The man had already pulled the gun from his waistband with his right hand. It had to be his right hand.

There was a flash of surprise in the Ranger's eyes, and a movement of his hand towards his own weapon. But he was too late, way too late, and he knew it.

The man squeezed the trigger, once, twice, and a third time. The Ranger rocked back in his seat, jerking under the impacts of the 9mm hollow point slugs. Then, as the light drained from his eyes, he slouched to one side, twitching slightly. Blood bubbled from the gunshot wounds as he fell from his seat and started to spasm. The man stood for a moment, watching. He had to be sure the Ranger was dead. The blood began to flow from his gaping mouth. It was done, but just to make sure, the man put a fourth bullet into the side of the Ranger's head. He smiled, dropped the gun and turned away.

The older woman who'd been seated at the counter was on the floor, hunched over, eyes wide, staring at him silently. The wait staff was nowhere to be seen, hiding, he presumed. Something crashed to the ground in the kitchen. The Mexican President was still on the TV.

The man turned and looked towards one of the security cameras. He was on an adrenaline high. He winked at the camera, turned to the front door and pushed it open with his right hand, then walked out of the restaurant. The deed was done. The plan had been executed with precision.

He got into his car, started the engine and removed the flesh-covered glove from his right hand, careful to do so below the dash, low enough that no stray camera could catch him doing it. Then he took his phone from his pocket and placed the call.

"It's done," he said.

"Good." The voice had a thick Latino accent. "Get rid of the car and go to the truck depot. Alberto will get you across."

"And my money?" He noticed the shake in his own voice. Was it fear? Or the rush of the kill? He couldn't be sure.

"You will get your money, my friend. All in due time. The trap has been set, but the lobo is still walking free. Just get rid of the car. And do not get caught."

"Right." He terminated the call. Now his hands were starting to shake.

It might have been his imagination, but he thought he heard sirens echoing in the night. He needed to get away, and quickly.

El Coco was right. The trap was set. But the wolf—the lobo—had no idea what was coming to him.

The lobo lived far away from Laredo. He'd never set foot in Texas. His name was Harry Starke.

1

Thursday, July 17, 2019

Chattanooga, Tennessee

Afternoon

The summer sun made little mirages on the highway as I drove into town that afternoon. The angle of the sun was just right—or maybe I should say wrong—because it probably would have blinded me if I hadn't been wearing the pair of reflective sunglasses I kept up in the visor.

I wasn't alone in the car, either. Amanda, my lovely wife, was seated next to me. Her head was tilted back, her eyes closed. It was hot outside, but inside the vehicle it was the perfect temperature for an afternoon nap. If I hadn't brought along a travel thermos of coffee—dark Italian roast—I'd have been dozing off, too.

Jade, our fourteen-month-old baby girl, was asleep in the back seat, rocking gently to the rumble of the drive, strapped safely in her car seat. Seated beside Jade was Maria Boylan, our live-in nanny and bodyguard.

Maria never sleeps... well, as far as I can tell. I glanced at her in my rearview mirror. She seemed to be at peace as she gazed out of the window, little wrinkles sprouting from the corners of her eyes like spiderwebs. Her face was beginning to show her years, but her eyes were sharp, always watching, always studying her surroundings. If you took her to be nothing more than Jade's nanny—which she was—you'd be seriously wrong. She was a coiled snake, always ready to strike. And her tongue was quick, too, quicker than most.

It was a perfect afternoon. Just about as perfect as I could imagine. Little did I know it was the perfect example of calm before the perfect storm.

We were on our way home from the cabin in northwest Georgia. Ten whole days in the woods, far away from the madding crowd, taking afternoon naps, reading by the fire pit, going for early morning hikes and enjoying evening picnics. It was just what the doctor ordered, literally. Doc Harrison had ordered me to get some R&R. In fact he'd threatened me, and I quote, "If you don't, I'll shoot you with a tranquilizer dart and keep you under for a week."

I've been shot before by bullets and darts alike, but I didn't take his threat seriously. I did, however, bow to his wisdom and planned an extended family vacation. And the doctor was right. I really did need to unplug for a while. We all did.

But now we were heading home, refreshed and reju-
venated, which was good because I was beginning to
become decidedly antsy. It was time to get back to work.
We had a lot of work to do to get Harry Starke Investigations up and running again after the destruction of my
offices on Georgia Avenue. *Damn you, Shady Tree.*

Shady Tree! I mused to the sound of the tires
humming hypnotically on the pavement. *No longer a
problem in my life. Not since he killed himself a month
ago...* It was that thought that triggered something deep in
my gut I couldn't quite grasp, and then Amanda opened
her eyes just as we started the climb up Lookout Mountain. She smiled at me and placed her hand on mine,
which was resting on the center console.

"What are you thinking about?" she asked.

"Nothing," I said and shot her a puzzled look. "What
makes you think I have something on my mind?"

"You were frowning, Harry. So what's up?"

I hadn't realized I was frowning. I shrugged. "I was...
just thinking things through. What I need to get done.
You know how it is. There's a lot of work to do. You and
Jade. Getting back to work. It's all, well, perfect."

Amanda nodded. "I know what you mean. But
Harry? About this getting back to work business. You're
going to find a new office, right? Going from that quiet
cabin to how things were before... I don't know if my
nerves can take that."

I nodded. "Finding new offices is at the top of my list,
Amanda. In fact, if I know Jacque, I'll bet she ignored my
orders to take a vacation like everyone else and has been
looking at properties the entire time we've been away."

I felt kind of sorry for Amanda. After the bomb demolished my office, I'd been determined to finish off every work commitment the agency had up to that point, and that meant buying new computers and equipment and making a temporary base of operations in our house on Lookout Mountain.

So, for the past few weeks, our lives had been turned upside down and then some. On top of that, of course, Amanda was still recovering from her car accident, and we had a newborn in the house... Well, not so newborn anymore. At least we had full-time help with her.

I looked at Maria in the rearview mirror. "Did you have fun this week, Maria?"

She glanced at me with that always-twinkling smile of hers. "You know I did, *mijo*. I haven't been out in the woods in a long time." She turned toward the still-sleeping Jade. "And this little angel made the whole vacation even better."

I smiled. Maria was a lifesaver. I already told you that I suspected the woman never slept. She was at hand to attend to Jade at all hours of the night, and she always knew what to do to comfort the baby. She rocked Jade or played with her or tickled her or fed her or sang to her with an inhuman combination of precision and grandmotherly care. I suppose having five kids and nine grandkids would do that to you—turn you into a baby-soothing machine.

Maria was quite a find—thanks again to Jacque Hale, my inimitable business partner and PA. I was confident that Maria, an ex-ATF agent, could handle just about every situation from changing a diaper to a full-blown shoot-out.

I heaved a long, self-satisfied sigh. "We should grill some steaks tonight. What do you think, Amanda?"

She nodded, squeezed my hand and said, "Good idea. I'll make a salad. Maria, can you help me?"

"Of course. I'll make a salsa."

My stomach twisted at the thought. One thing about having Maria around was the never-ending parade of spicy foods she liked to prepare. I thought I liked salsa before, but my gut was starting to protest the daily torture. But I just smiled. It made the woman happy, so why not? I'd just have a little. It was always so tasty.

"We should invite your father," Amanda added. "I'm sure Rose is going crazy not seeing Jade for more than a week."

"Agreed," I said. It was a good plan, and at just the right time because we were pulling up the drive to our house.

I can't tell you I was surprised to see Jacque walk out the front door, a big smile on her face. She was one of the few people that knew exactly when we were coming home, and aside from my father and Kate, she was the only other person that knew the access codes to get into my house whenever she wanted.

I was barely out of the truck when Jacque started laughing. "Why, Harry. You so look like you enjoyed your romp in the woods. You've never looked happier. And you've put on a few pounds, I see."

I looked down at my gut, frowning, when I realized she was joking. At least I hoped she was joking. The last thing I wanted was to get a bad case of *dad bod*, even if I was now a father.

"Hello, Jacque," Amanda called.

Maria was gently waking Jade and unstrapping her from the car seat.

"It's good to see you, Jacque," I said. And I meant it. "But I gotta say: you don't look like a woman on vacation."

She shrugged, her smooth, caramel features shining with joy. "I guess you caught me at dat. I've just been hunting for new offices, is all. I bin buggin' every real estate agent in town, but I have some good options for you to look at tomorrow. Some places dat are just perfect, plus a little room to grow."

I liked the sound of that. And I always got a kick out of the sound of Jacque's Jamaican accent, too. She usually used it when she was scolding me. I wondered what I'd done this time.

Maria passed Jade off to Amanda. "You take this bundle of joy, ma'am, and I'll help with the bags."

"Thank you, Maria," Amanda said, almost absent-mindedly as she looked down at Jade, a motherly smile on her face. "And please stop calling me ma'am. Call me Amanda."

Maria frowned but nodded.

"Sounds good, Jacque," I said. "But we can talk all about that tomorrow, can't we?"

"Of course," was Jacque's answer. "I just left some files on your kitchen table so you can look them over. You'd have already seen the pictures if you bothered to check your phone."

"Oh, right," I said and reached through the open car door and thumbed open the glove box. My iPhone was inside. Don't get me wrong. I hadn't left it there the whole ten days at the cabin. I'd turned it on once or twice. But I'd really wanted to get away this last week, and that meant no emails or phone calls.

As the iPhone started up, I waved at Jacque, who was walking out to her car.

"See you tomorrow, Harry."

"Thanks, Jacque." The text messages popped up right away, complete with pictures of buildings and offices. But something else caught my eye, too. Four missed calls from Kate.

I looked at the call record, frowning. All four calls had come in the last fifteen minutes. Talk about timing.

"Harry," Amanda said. "Aren't you going to help Maria with the luggage?"

I looked up, an apology on my face, but I was too distracted to answer her. I had a bad feeling swirling around in my gut, and it wasn't the kind of bad feeling you get from eating too much of Maria's salsa. Something wasn't right.

Four missed calls? What was so urgent? The last one was just three minutes ago. I hesitated for a second. Should I call her right back? Or just wait for her to call again, which I figured would be any minute.

Turned out I didn't need to do either.

A roaring engine and squealing tires echoed from behind me. It was loud, too. Loud enough to stop Jacque in her tracks, just as she was about to circle down the drive.

Suddenly, as the roaring reached a peak, Kate's unmarked cruiser came speeding around the corner and up the drive. She skidded—I mean literally skidded—to a stop behind my Range Rover and jumped out of the car.

"Kate?" I managed to say. But my mind was racing at this point. What was going on? Was someone hurt? An image came to my mind of my father, August Starke, lying dead somewhere in a pool of his own blood. Had something happened to him? No, it couldn't be that, because Rose would have called us before Kate did. So what was going on? Whatever it was, it had to be bad.

The look on Kate's face didn't make me feel any better, either. Her eyes were wide. She looked scared, but she looked angry, too. Was she mad at me? Kate and I used to be what you'd call an item, years ago, and I knew what it was like to have her mad at me. What had I done this time?

"Harry," Kate said breathlessly. "We're going to figure this out. I don't know what happened, but we're going to get you out of this, and we're going to get whoever did it."

"Kate," I said, stepping toward her. "Calm down. You're not making any sense. Take a breath. Tell me what happened. What the hell's going on?"

That's when I heard the sirens. Multiple police cars, from the sound of it, heading this way. But why?

"They're coming for you, Harry," Kate said. "They're coming to arrest you."

"Arrest him?" Amanda said. "You can't be serious, Kate."

"Oh, but I am. They'll be here any minute."

"Why would they arrest me?" I asked. I'd been at the cabin for the last ten days, for Pete's sake. "What's the charge, Kate?"

Kate's eyes narrowed and her voice dropped two octaves as she replied, "Murder!"

Thursday, July 17, 2019

Afternoon

"M urder?" I blurted. "What the hell?"

Kate nodded, obviously without words herself. Amanda, holding Jade, just looked at me, her face pale.

"How is that possible?" I said. "I haven't killed anybody."

Even as I said the words, I knew they weren't true. I'd killed before. More than once, in fact, but I'd always managed to stay on the right side of the law. Well, almost always.

Images of Duvon James lying on that couch came flooding back to me. I remembered him looking up at me as I surprised him. I was so angry that night. Amanda was in the ICU, and we didn't know if she was going to make it. He pulled his weapon, and I shot him dead. I remembered taking that plane over the lake, the water still boiling from the heat of the nuclear blast. And I shoved the body out of the aircraft and watched as it tumbled into the water. Nothing of him would have been left. Nothing recognizable, anyway.

But no one knew about that, other than me and the pilot, and he would never talk. And, technically, it was above-board, anyway—self-defense.

But could someone else have pieced it together? Was that what this was all about? I had no way of knowing.

Maria came around the back of the Range Rover. "If you plan to run, Harry, I know some people. They can keep you safe."

I looked at her. I'm embarrassed to say that I actually considered it, if only for a split second. Thankfully, my better judgment won out. That, and the stern looks I got from both Kate and Amanda. Running wasn't an option, and I told Maria that.

I looked back at Kate. "I'll cooperate, Kate. You know that, but someone has to be behind this."

Kate nodded. The sirens grew louder. Closer. Within a few seconds, the first of the police cars turned into the drive and came to a stop behind Kate's unmarked cruiser.

The second car to pull in was another unmarked vehicle, one I recognized, not as an undercover police cruiser, but as Chief Johnston's personal car, an ocean blue Honda Accord.

Behind him were two more blue and white cruisers, their lights flashing, sirens blaring. It was quite the entourage.

My mind was still spinning as the police officers exited the vehicles, men and women I knew, most of them. Thankfully, none of them drew their weapons or took aggressive stances. That was probably because Kate had already moved closer to me, her hands out, showing there was no cause for concern.

When Police Chief Johnston climbed out of his car—he's a big man—he was scowling, a deeper scowl than the one he liked to wear most of the time. It was a serious look, even for this serious man. And he was looking right at me.

What had I done to deserve all this manpower? I mean, seriously. My front drive now looked like something out of a TNT police drama, one in which I was the bad guy they arrest at the end of the episode.

There was a tiny part of my soul that still hoped this was some kind of practical joke, something Jacque and Kate had organized. A surprise birthday party, perhaps? It wasn't even close to my birthday though.

And Johnston would never condone such a frivolous and showy display of police force—especially in my neighborhood. And he certainly wouldn't have attended himself. We aren't on the worst of terms these days, not like we were a couple of years ago, but Johnston and I weren't exactly best buds. I would call our present relationship one of mutual respect. That being so, if he had deigned to leave the comfort of his office, whatever was going on was... serious.

And then I noticed Johnston had two other men with him. When they got out of the car, it became clear that this was no surprise stunt. I still didn't know what it was, but I knew I was in big trouble.

The first of the two men, the tallest, was aged about fifty. He wore a gray, bushy mustache that just about qualified as a handlebar. He was thin as a rail, wore blue jeans and a button-down shirt, no tie, and a tan sports jacket. On top of that, he carried a cowboy hat that was just a few shades darker than his jacket.

The second man was shorter and heavier. Not fat. Muscular. His arms bulged under the long-sleeved, dark green button-down shirt. He wore a matching greenish-blue tie, held in place by a brass tie clip. He also wore jeans and a belt with a buckle that had to weigh two pounds. He was clean-shaven, but his sideburns, thick and brown, stretched down to the bottom of his jaw. He, too, was holding a cowboy hat.

Both men were armed, their weapons visible on their belts.

And they both wore cowboy boots, brown leather with swirly designs sewn into the sides, just visible beneath the hems of the jeans.

The man in the lead—how could he be comfortable wearing a jacket in this summer heat?—put on his hat and took out a wallet and badge. I thought at first that the metal star with a circle around it looked like a US Marshal's badge, but then I saw it was missing the American eagle in the center, and that's when I noticed the words printed on the edge of the badges.

They're Texas Rangers? What are they doing all the way up here? And, more importantly, what do they want with me?

"Harry Starke?" the lead Ranger said. "My name is
Captain David Culp of the Texas Rangers, Company D.
This is my partner, Lieutenant John Booth. And we're
here to take you into custody, pending transfer to the
State of Texas. Have you been informed of your rights?"

I shook my head. "No, I haven't. But I was told the
charge is murder. May I ask who the hell I'm supposed to
have murdered all the way down in Texas?"

"We can talk about that down at the police station,"
Culp said, his Texas drawl dripping off his every word.
"Chief, if your officers will handle the arrest, we'd be
much obliged."

Texans are usually typecast as slow talkers, and Culp
was no exception. Every word he said was stretched out,
as if he had all the time in the world.

Johnston nodded at Culp, then looked at me and said,
"I'm sorry about this, Starke. I'm sure you'll be able to
straighten it out, either here or in Laredo." He motioned
for two of the police officers to make the arrest.

Kate stepped up next to me and put an arm on my
shoulder. "I'll do it, Chief."

Johnston stared at her for a long moment, then finally
nodded and said, "Fine. But Wallace will ride along with
you to the police department."

I saw the look Kate flashed Chief Johnston. It was a
look that could have made the arctic ice cap melt and
then come to a roaring boil in thirty seconds flat. But she
didn't say anything.

Of course, I knew what she was thinking. Johnston
didn't trust her to get me to the police department. Did
he really think she'd go AWOL over me, ruining her

career and making my situation even worse than it already was? Not frickin' likely.

Kate turned away from the crowd and looked at me. "I'm going to have to handcuff you, Harry. I'm really sorry about this."

"They have a warrant?" I asked.

"Yeah, they do."

"Then you don't have a choice, Kate. Just get on with it."

And she did.

As she went through all the steps and advised me of my rights, I turned to Amanda and told her I loved her. She had tears in her eyes, but she stood tall and strong and said she loved me, too. I'd never adored that woman more than I did in that moment. I called to Jacque to get on the phone with my father, and TJ and Tim, but she was already on it without my having to ask. Jacque's a sharp one. Always has been.

I knew I hadn't done anything to deserve this Texas Ranger treatment. I was being framed, obviously, but I trusted my father and my team to get me out of the mess I'd suddenly found myself in. In the meantime, I just had to keep my head down and my ears open.

A couple of minutes later, I was in the back of Kate's car with Officer Wallace riding shotgun. He didn't look any happier about being there than I was. The police entourage followed, quiet this time, lights on but no sirens. I figured the sirens were for the benefit of the two Texans riding with Johnston. The Chief had to make a big show of it. If the warrant was from out of state, which I figured it had to be, that meant it had been issued by a federal judge, probably somebody important. I didn't blame Johnston for coming along.

"Kate, can't you tell me anything about what I'm facing here?" I asked from the back seat. "I mean, I've been out at the cabin for the last ten days, for crying out loud."

"I know it, Harry. I wish I had something to tell you, but I really don't know much more than you do. These two Texas Rangers just showed up at the police department this morning. Johnston talked to them for a long time in his office. He even raised his voice. I think he defended you, Harry, and I think he tried to get the warrant thrown out. But it didn't work."

I leaned back in the seat and stared out the window. "Right," I said.

"All I know is that someone in Laredo, Texas, is dead," she continued, "and these guys are convinced you're the one who pulled the trigger."

I frowned. Something was bothering me, but I couldn't put my finger on it.

"I wish I knew more. I really do," Kate said.

"Don't worry, Kate. It's fine. My team will get to the bottom of this."

It's something about Laredo, isn't it? I thought.

I couldn't quite put my finger on it, but something felt oddly familiar. But what?

We pulled into the parking lot at the police department, and guess who was standing outside? None other than Henry "Tiny" Finkle, his arms crossed, looking at me with a self-satisfied grin.

"Well, well, well," he said as Kate let me out of the

unmarked cruiser and walked me into the building. "Looks like all your shenanigans have finally caught up with you, huh, Starke?"

"Cut it out, Finkle," I said. "Even you're smart enough to know I didn't sneak down to Texas to kill anyone."

"Oh, sure. You say that now, but you've straddled that line for far too long, Starke. I think Karma's finally catching up with you."

As the booking process continued, Kate apologetic at every step, I couldn't help but wonder if Tiny was right. I mean, maybe I was being framed. But did I deserve this? I'd skirted the line plenty of times, but I'm pretty sure I never actually crossed it. It just isn't in me to go around offing people, even if they are bad guys.

My pockets emptied, prints taken, and mug shots snapped, Kate walked me back to lockup. The door clicked shut and, for the first time in a long while, I found myself inside a cell.

"You'll get out of this, Harry," Kate said. "I know you. You're slipperier than a soaped-up eel. You'll get to the bottom of it."

She turned away and suddenly I was alone.

I walked to the back of the cell and sat down on the bunk. *How many bad guys have I thrown in here, I wonder? And now here I am... If only I knew what the charges were, exactly. Who the hell am I supposed to have killed?*

Then it hit me, like the proverbial brick.

Shady!

I suddenly remembered that Lester "Shady" Tree

had spent some time—a lot of time—working with the Mexican cartels. I'd heard that months ago. The next time I saw him, he was helping terrorists plant a nuclear device in downtown Chattanooga. *But where was it he'd been? Laredo! That was it, Laredo. No. It was Nuevo Laredo, the Mexican sister to Laredo, Texas.*

I shook my head. It couldn't be a coincidence. I'd been set up. *And by Shady Tree, no less, even though he was now dead. Oh yeah, Shady promised me it wasn't over, even as he pulled the trigger and blew his own brains out. What was it he said?*

"You've lost, Harry. You just don't know it yet. Even after I'm gone. I'm the Pacman, remember? I always get my man. We still have to play the end game. Goodbye, Harry."

Oh yeah, something like that. And then the son of a bitch smiled at me and put the barrel of the gun into his mouth and pulled the trigger.

So, I thought, smiling ruefully to myself, *it begins. Now we play the end game.*

3

Thursday, July 17, 2019

Late afternoon

It was probably less than an hour later—although I couldn't be sure because they'd confiscated both my watch and iPhone as part of the booking process—when I was taken out of the cell and led to one of the interrogation rooms. A young officer—one I didn't know—cuffed me and led me from the cell, his hand gingerly on my arm. He didn't say a word, but I could tell he was embarrassed that he had to do it. Many of the cops, people I knew, some of whom I'd worked with back in the day when I was a detective for the Chattanooga PD, looked away as I walked by. All except Kate, who watched with wide eyes from across the room, and Henry Finkle, who watched with a broad grin on his face.

Everyone else seemed more embarrassed to see me in handcuffs than I was.

"If you'll just wait in here, Mr. Starke," the young cop said in a soft, hesitant voice before leaving me alone in the interrogation room.

I looked around the room for a moment, and I couldn't help but smile grimly at the irony of it all. I knew this room like the back of my own hand. I'd been in here dozens—perhaps even hundreds—of times.

The room was small. No fancy stainless steel table and wall-sized one-way mirror like you see on TV. This room wasn't much bigger than a closet. I glanced up at the cameras located near the ceiling in two corners. Both were on. Small red lights confirming they were recording both video and audio. They wouldn't have left me alone if they weren't.

The table was plain, simple, and anchored to the floor. I sat down in one of the chairs and looked across the table, waiting for someone to come in and start hammering me with questions.

I knew the procedure. They wanted to sweat me first. I couldn't blame them. It was textbook, a tactic that sometimes worked. Well, it sometimes worked on the guilty. But I wasn't guilty. Yep, I knew all the tricks. I'd used them myself, too many times to remember.

How many times have I been in this very room, looking drug dealers or murderers or witnesses in the eyes? I wondered. *How many times have Kate and I played tag team on a suspect, her asking the questions and me studying their faces as they answered?*

I used to believe I could spot a lie more accurately

than a lie detector. Since then, I've wised up, a lot. People, all people, are born predators, wily predators. It's part of human nature. I came to realize some people can hide the truth even from me, though not very often. I've learned to expect the unexpected.

But this? Being framed for murder by a dead man? It was a bit of a shocker.

Even in the years since I'd left the force, I'd been in that room several times, helping with investigations. Or, sometimes, running my own investigation parallel to whatever the police were doing.

But today I was on the wrong side of the table. I was the one that was about to be interviewed. Now I was the suspect. And I have to tell you, it's not a nice feeling being on the wrong side of the table.

Then again, the fact that the Texas Rangers wanted to talk to me at all was fine in my book. The sooner Culp and his muscular sidekick came around to ask me their questions, the sooner I'd be able to get some answers to questions of my own. And I had quite a list, let me tell you.

Who did I supposedly kill in Texas?

When did the murder happen?

What evidence did they have against me?

How did Shady manage to arrange it all? How did he manage to frame me after he was dead and buried?

Okay, that last question was a long shot, and I didn't expect the Texas Rangers to know anything about Lester Tree and his personal vendetta against me and my family, but what the hell? I knew damn well that Shady was behind it. Just how, exactly... I had no frickin' idea.

The door opened and I held my breath. *Time to get this show on the road.*

But it wasn't Captain David Culp, or any other police officer, that entered the room. It was my father.

August Starke walked into the room dressed in a dark gray suit, a white shirt with a navy-blue collar, a plain navy-blue tie and black shoes that literally glistened. Not a hair was out of place. And his expression was ice cold, totally professional.

You might have expected him—being my father—to be something of a wreck, discovering that his son had been arrested for murder. But August is more than just my father. He's also one of the greatest legal minds in the country. Sure, his expertise is in tort and not criminal law, but, as he sat down beside me, a slim briefcase in his hand, there was no one else in the world I'd rather have had at my side.

"What have they told you, Harry?" August's voice was low, just above a whisper, but sharp. He'd brought his A-game.

I love you too, Dad.

"Not much, to be honest. Only that I supposedly killed someone in Texas."

"Who was the victim?"

I shrugged.

"When was the murder?"

"No idea."

August nodded slowly. I couldn't hold back a smile. He was asking the same questions I wanted answers to. *Great minds really do think alike.*

A half beat later, the door opened again and in

walked Culp and his partner, Lieutenant John Booth. They were dressed as before, but minus the cowboy hats. Culp carried what looked like an iPad in his hand.

"Mr. Starke, and, uh, Mr. Starke, is it?" Culp asked.

August put out his hand and Culp shook it.

"That's right, my name is August Starke. For the time being, I'll be representing my son. You must have some questions for Harry. But we also have some questions for you."

I couldn't be sure, but I thought I saw a smile under Culp's big mustache. "I'm sure you do. Let's get down to brass tacks, shall we?"

Booth shook August's hand and introduced himself. Then the two Texas Rangers sat down opposite us, and Culp flipped open the cover on the iPad and displayed an image, tilting the tablet up to show me.

It was an image of a gun, a Heckler & Koch VP9, to be exact. Just like the one I carried, up until a month ago.

My eyebrows shot right up.

"Do you recognize this weapon, Mr. Starke?" David Culp asked me.

My eyes narrowed. I looked at him. *Just what kind of game is this guy playing?*

"Well, I recognize the kind of weapon, sure. It's a VP9."

Culp nodded. "Is this a weapon you normally carry, Mr. Starke?"

I glanced at my father. He didn't look at me; instead his steel-gray eyes were boring into Culp's head.

"What kind of nonsense is this, Captain?" August said before I could answer.

Culp raised a hand in defense. "Mr. Starke, uh, sir. You know as well as I do that I'm not asking your son to say anything incriminating. I'm just trying to get a handle on things, okay?"

After a long moment, August nodded and looked at me.

"Yeah, I'm sure plenty of people could tell you that, until a few weeks ago, I used to carry a VP9. Now I carry a CZ Shadow."

"You've owned several VP9s over the years, I'm sure."

"That's true." What I didn't tell the man is that many of my weapons had been confiscated and logged away in the PD evidence room. Sometimes I got them back. Sometimes I didn't. There were several I hadn't seen in a good long time.

"Now, I don't expect you to memorize the serial numbers on every gun registered to you or your company, but, I should show you this." Culp swiped on the iPad showing another shot of the same weapon, the serial number clearly visible.

Culp looked up from the iPad, studying my face. I knew that look. He was looking for the tell, the one that would let him know that I was about to lie... or not.

I didn't know if it was one of my weapons or not, so I said nothing.

"Would it surprise you to know that this particular weapon is registered to you, Mr. Starke?"

"Don't answer that, Harry," August said. "Cut to the chase, Captain."

I have to tell you, I was shocked and confused. And I'm sure the Lone Ranger and Tonto seated on the other side of the table could see clearly that I was, and that I had no idea what the hell was going on.

"This particular weapon," Culp said, swiping once again on the tablet screen, "was used in a murder in Laredo, Texas, a few days ago. Can you tell me how your weapon got down to Texas, son?"

The next image on the iPad was the kind of scene I was all too familiar with. A man lying on the floor in what looked to be some kind of restaurant. He was staring up at the ceiling, his eyes lifeless, blood pooling around him from several gunshot wounds in the stomach, chest, and head.

"Do not say anything else, Harry," August said.

Culp nodded gravely. "That would be wise counsel to follow, Mr. Starke. So, how about you just listen for a minute? This man's name is... was Cory Sloan. He is..." Culp's voice cracked for just a second. "He was a major in the Texas Rangers. He headed the Laredo office. He was a good man."

"You're telling me my gun was used to kill this man?" I blurted.

My father looked at me, silently commanding me to shut up. But I was just too upset to give a damn anymore. How could this be happening to me? I'd never been to Texas. I kept thinking that again and again. *I've never even been there. How can this be possible?*

I leaned forward in my chair, speaking again before either Culp or my father could say a word.

"When did this murder take place?"

"Last Thursday," Culp said. "The twelfth."

"Well, there you have it," I said. "I was out at my

cabin in northwest Georgia last Thursday. Been there all week. More than a week, in fact."

"And you have evidence to that effect?" Lieutenant John Booth, who'd been sitting, silent, with his thick arms folded across his chest, said. He stared at me with eyes that were... well, the only way to describe them is that they were too blue. Just too damn blue to be real. They were almost surreal, as if he was some kind of robot. "Can anyone corroborate it?"

Culp shot Booth a hard look. The younger man, lower in rank, was obviously not supposed to talk during this interview.

"Yes," I said. "I was out there with my wife and Maria, my daughter's nanny."

Booth didn't break eye contact with me, ignoring Culp's look. Instead, his face seemed to get redder. "So your wife and an employee. Don't sound like reliable alibis to me, Mr. Starke." He practically spat the final words.

Culp raised a hand, signaling for Booth to stop.

I was angry. I wasn't used to being treated like that. I leaned forward and opened my mouth to speak, but my father, mirroring Culp's movements, raised a hand to settle me.

"I don't know how you gentlemen do things down in Texas," August said, his voice calm but cold and calculating, "but I encourage you to check out my client's alibi before condemning him."

Culp looked at Booth for a long moment. Booth finally looked down, tearing his eyes away from mine. *Is this guy emotional? It seems like it to me.*

Finally, Culp looked back at my father, then at me. "You'll have to excuse my partner here. But I'm afraid no alibi will prevent you from being transferred to Laredo for arraignment."

"This is insane," I said. "All because a gun registered to me was found at the scene? One of many I own and have owned, I might add."

Culp nodded. "I understand your frustration, Mr. Starke. But there is more. Much more."

He swiped again on the iPad. The next file wasn't an image. It was a video clip.

And that video clip gave me the shock of my life.

The clip was short and low quality, typical surveillance camera footage. I had to lean forward and squint to make sure I could see what was happening.

A man wearing a baseball cap came into the restaurant. It was a Denny's, I realized from the video.

The place was just about empty. Only one customer. Baseball cap sat down and ordered. Then the Texas Ranger in the previous image of the crime scene walked in. Culp had said his name was Cory Sloan, an older man, based on what I saw. Except at the time the video was being recorded, he wasn't dead. He took a seat at a table at one end of the restaurant, minding his own business.

Then the man wearing the ball cap stood and walked up to Major Sloan. He seemed almost nonchalant as he pulled a pistol from the back of his waistband and leveled it at the Texas Ranger.

Sloan noticed the gun too late. He barely made a move before Mr. Baseball Cap opened fire.

I watched as three bullets tore into the Ranger's body.

Then the shooter stood over the Ranger, looking down at him as if to make sure the man was dead, shot him once in the head, and then casually dropped the gun. It was impossible to tell in the video, but the gun looked to me to be a VP9. Whether or not it was the one from the previous photos, the one Culp insisted was registered to me, I had no idea. But big deal! So someone stole one of my guns and took it to Texas and killed someone. Doesn't mean it was me.

Wait a damn minute...

The shooter turned and walked to the exit. Before he left, however, he turned and looked up at the security camera. Yeah, he actually looked up at it, right at the camera. And then he winked.

I felt all the blood drain from my face.

How was it possible?

The video ended when the shooter turned to the exit and pushed open the door.

I tore my eyes away from the iPad and looked at my father.

Now, August Starke is a courtroom genius. He's seen everything. In fact, he's made more than a billion dollars from the cases he's won. Part of his success comes from the fact that he believes he's the smartest person in the room. And most of the time, he is. But now... even he was speechless.

Because the man in the video was me.

4

Thursday, July 17, 2019

Late afternoon

The man in that video, in that Denny's, in Laredo, Texas, murdering a Texas Ranger, was... me.

I was stunned, flabbergasted; there's no other way to say it. It was as if I was looking in the mirror.

He had the same build. The same shaped face and features, but more than that, he even had my eyes.

"Now maybe you can see why you're going to Texas, Mr. Starke," Culp said quietly. "That's you in this video. True, the quality is crap, but we have our best techs working on it down in Austin, improving the resolution, making blown-up images of your face as we speak. Because that is your face, isn't it, Mr. Starke? Your face, your build, and your gun, and you can't deny it."

I was speechless. I leaned back, putting my hands on the back of my head.

"I... I... I do deny that's me. I categorically deny it. I've never been to Texas in my life."

Culp gave a firm nod. "So you've said."

Booth leaned forward in his seat, staring at me once again. "Your prints are on the gun, Starke. No one else's. Just yours. You wanna change your story now? Make it easier on all of us?"

I looked at my father, shaking my head. "I was at the cabin all week," I said weakly.

"Harry," August said, his voice almost a whisper, "please listen to me." His eyes were dead serious. And I mean D-E-A-D, dead serious. I'm sure he was thinking about capital punishment. The image of me strapped to a bed, all prepped and ready to receive the lethal injection, yelling over and over that I didn't do it.

My father's next words were quiet but firm, the words of a man that meant business. "Do not say another word."

He looked at the two Texas Rangers. "Can we please have the room? I need to confer with my client."

Booth smirked. "I'm sure you do."

Culp shot his partner a dirty look, then looked back at my father and me. "Fine, but before we go, you should know two final things. First, DNA was found on your gun, Mr. Starke. It's being rushed through the lab now and will be back by the end of the week. Considering your prints are on the weapon, we don't doubt the DNA will match yours. We also have a flight in your name from Nashville to DFW to San Antonio, as well as car rentals out of the San Antonio International Airport."

"We understand," August said. I could tell he was becoming more and more uncomfortable.

Me? I was a wreck. But I tried to look calm. I wasn't sure if I was succeeding though.

"That was the first thing," Culp continued. "The second thing is this. We've already run a ballistics search from this gun, and the firearm's unique ballistic markings match a drug-related multiple-victim execution from a couple of months ago."

August pulled out his phone, making a note. "When was this?"

Culp gave him a date, and my heart sank.

It was Shady. I now had no doubt about it. And, oh, was he good. My gun. My doppelganger. It was all too perfect, but the prior execution? That was the cherry on top.

It was the day I shot and killed Duvon James, the man that ran Amanda off the road, nearly killed her and the baby—our baby—still in her womb.

It was the day I confronted James, the day he pulled a weapon on me, the day I ended his life. The day I got Jimmy Little to take me and James's body up into the air and over the lake. The day I dumped the body into water that was still boiling from the sub-aquatic nuclear explosion.

No one knew about what I did that day. No one but me and Jimmy.

But—somehow—Shady knew. Boy was he smart. He'd set this up, probably months ago. Probably right after we took a pair of bolt cutters to his finger to get the information from him we needed to save the city.

The Texas Rangers left the room, and August stared up at the camera in the corner until it flicked off and we were officially alone.

"Right," he said. "You'll need a lawyer in Texas. I'll make some phone calls."

"You can't be my lawyer?" I asked. I already knew the answer to that question, but it's amazing what stress will do to your ability to think straight.

August shook his head. "You need a criminal defense lawyer. And you need someone who's licensed to practice law in Texas." He pursed his lips. "I can and will be there and offer support, but you need someone to represent you in court. I'll make some phone calls. We'll find the best, no matter the cost."

"Fine."

"Harry, they will check your alibi," August continued. "They'll probably subpoena Amanda and Maria, and they'll want a detailed accounting of your movements on the days of both this murder and the other killing a few months ago."

I nodded but didn't say anything. A detailed accounting for the day I dropped a nuclear device into the lake? Shady knew what he was doing when he set it up. That was also the day TJ and I tortured—I mean interrogated—Shady, and later found Duvon James, ended his life, and dumped his body into the still-boiling lake.

I couldn't say any of that. I couldn't drag TJ and Jimmy into that mess. I'd just get them both thrown in jail. Not to mention the fact that I'd get off the hook for one murder just to end up on trial for a different one.

Duvon James had pulled a weapon on me. I knew that, and my conscience was clear, but there was no way I'd ever be able to prove it.

"What are you thinking about?" August asked me.

I realized I'd been lost in thought.

"My mind's in a whirl. I hate what this will do to Amanda and Jade and my team." It wasn't a lie, exactly. I was thinking all kinds of other things, but my family and friends were high on my list of anxieties.

I leaned on my elbows, looking down at the tabletop.

"This is all down to Shady, Dad. I know it."

August looked confused. "Lester Tree? Didn't he kill himself a month ago?"

"Yes, he did, but he told me something before he died. I never told anyone this before. No one else knows, except Tim, and he knows only because he was listening in on the comms. But it's the only thing I can think of."

"What did he say, Harry?"

"He told me that he'd won, that he'd get me. And that even after he was gone, he'd beat me."

August shook his head, dismissing it. "No, that's just wild talk. He was just trying to psych you out. Surely you've heard people talk like that before?"

"Yeah, but this was different. I'm telling you, Dad. Shady had this weird look in his eyes. It was as if he knew he'd win. And the autopsy showed that he was sick, cancer. He'd only had a couple of months left to live, anyway."

August was quiet, thinking. But I was too impatient to let him think it through.

"I'm telling you. This has Shady written all over it. Who else would go to so much trouble to frame me? And all the way down there in Texas, where Shady had been living prior to the terrorist attack. It has to be him. There's no other answer."

"All right, Harry. I'll look into it. I trust your judgment. But we can't do much of anything before we find you a lawyer. I'll make arrangements and we'll meet again in Texas. We'll have access to their files. They'll have to share what they have, and we'll pick it apart."

I nodded. "Right."

"The tapes may have been altered," he said thoughtfully. "That must be how someone made it look like you were there."

"Tim will be able to help," I said.

August frowned. "It will need to be someone non-biased. We can't risk whatever Tim might find being thrown out of court."

Oh, right. I leaned back. My father was making sense.

"We'll find someone. Don't you worry about that. We'll attack hard right out of the gate and see if we can get it dismissed. But son, if it does go to trial, you need to be prepared."

"Prepared for what?"

"Every detail of your life will be picked apart by the prosecution. They'll dig deep, and they'll question everything you've ever done. You need to be ready for that. If this goes to trial, it will be long and bloody. Do you understand?"

I did.

"I'm going to leave now. I need to have an attorney in place when you arrive in Laredo. I'll be in touch as soon as I know something. Stay calm and keep your mouth shut. Don't let them goad you into saying something they can hang you with. Goodbye, son."

I nodded and August left the room. He was immediately replaced by the same young officer as before, who escorted me back to my cell.

Once there, I sat down on the bed and commenced to try to figure it all out. I was in a mess. No doubt about that and, at that point, it seemed damn near hopeless. Looking at it all objectively, they had me dead to rights. Had I been the investigating officer, I would have done exactly the same. I'd have thrown me in the can and tossed away the key.

So how do I handle it?

I'd always tried to stay within the law, but the thought of a Texas prosecutor going through my every case made my stomach churn.

On the other hand, though, how many times had Tim gotten information via... well, let's just say, less than legal means? Was I ready for every detail of my life to be picked apart by some over-eager prosecutor, not to mention the judge, jury, and everyone in the crowd, watching? Not only no, but hell no.

I understood what my father had said, but I also understood what he wasn't saying. He didn't say my team couldn't help me, just that whatever Tim might find wouldn't be admissible in court. At least, that's what I thought he meant.

I stood and began pacing my cell, my mind racing. The first thing I had to do was figure out how Shady had managed to pull it off.

How did he get hold of my gun?

My fingerprints?

My DNA? Assuming it was mine, which I figured was probably the case.

And who's helping Shady now? The guy's dead and in the ground. Someone with a lot of tech know-how altered the security video to make the shooter look like me. Who would go to all this trouble after Shady was dead and gone? A friend? A relative? Did he pay someone? If so, who?

"Too many unknowns." I growled in frustration.

I did know one thing, however. I'd need my team's help to figure all this out. I wasn't about to sit in a cell in Texas and wait for every case, every split-second decision, every mistake I'd made to be paraded publicly in front of a jury. Too much of what my team and I do dances in the gray area, and the wrong judge could decide to paint all the gray pure black, landing me and half my team in prison for decades. Not to mention all the court convictions that the Chattanooga PD would have to dig up and review. If I got blasted as a crooked investigator by a prosecutor with an attitude problem, that could affect every case I ever worked as a cop, all those years ago.

I sat down, hard, on the bunk. Shady really had done a number on me this time, and we had to unravel his trap... Fast.

5

Thursday, July 17, 2019

Evening

The hours passed, painfully slowly. Now and again a cop came by to gawk, pretending he, or she, had something important to do that necessitated they pass by my cell. I could already see the mood of the police department changing. At first, most of the men and women, people that had known me for a long time, were compassionate. Most of them assumed I was innocent. But I knew how the system worked. As the hours passed, some of them would begin talking among themselves. Doubts would sprout like weeds.

Maybe he did do it, some were probably thinking. He always was a contrary son of a bitch. Maybe he did fly down to Texas and kill someone. A fellow cop, no less.

If that's the kind of thinking I was facing, in a police

department that knew me, a department I had once been a part of, how the hell would it be in Texas? Geez, I didn't even want to think about it.

The cell door opened, interrupting my thoughts.

"Hey, you. How are you doing?" Kate asked.

"Hey, Kate. I'm okay, I guess."

She looked exhausted.

She stepped inside and closed the door.

"I'm sorry, Harry," she said. "I tried to get it pushed back. I talked to Johnston. I yelled and I pleaded, but the Texans have already gotten a van. You're leaving for Laredo first thing in the morning."

"Don't worry about it, Kate. You did what you could and I appreciate it."

I have to admit, I wasn't looking forward to a long drive down to South Texas in the back of a van. How long would it take? Two days, two and a half?

There was a knock on the door.

"I brought someone to see you," Kate said, turning to the door and opening it to reveal an officer. With him was Amanda, carrying our baby girl.

I smiled, and I'd be lying if I told you my eyes were completely dry. Tears were rolling down Amanda's cheeks. Even Kate's eyes were watering. The only one smiling was Jade.

"Oh, Harry," Amanda said as she grabbed me with her free hand. I put my arms around them both and kissed her and then Jade.

I glanced at the officer. His face was stoic. I nodded at him, then looked at Kate, but she shook her head. She knew what I wanted, but it wasn't going to happen. She'd get nothing but hell if she stepped outside and closed that cell door. It must have taken an act of congress for her to get Amanda and Jade in, anyway. For that, I would be eternally grateful, bless her.

I tickled Jade and her smile grew even bigger.

Amanda looked up at me, her eyes wide. "They tell me they're taking you to Texas tomorrow."

"That's what I hear," I said.

"I'm going too, Harry. Maria will come with me. I'll book flights for first thing in the morning."

"No, Amanda. You need to stay here."

She looked at me like I'd slapped her.

"I'm serious."

Kate stepped forward. "I'll be going, too, Harry. I already talked to Chief Johnston and he agreed."

I shook my head. "I appreciate that, Kate. I really do. But I think you all need to stay here."

Amanda looked like she was about to melt. "But why not? We need to be with you. To support you."

"No. Like I said, I appreciate it. But I think something else is going on."

"What do you mean?" Kate asked.

"I mean I think Shady Tree is behind this. He's framing me. This is an attack."

Kate's eyebrows just about jumped off her head. "Shady? But he's dead."

I caught them up briefly, sharing only the most pertinent details. I explained why I was sure that Shady Tree had orchestrated the frame before he died.

"I'm telling you," I said. "Shady's behind it. And I

don't know what else is in store. But you have to stay here and stay safe."

Amanda was shocked into silence. I was sure the thought of Shady attacking me from beyond the grave was bringing back the worst of her memories.

Kate stepped forward, concern on her face. "So you think there's more to come? That this is just the beginning?"

"I don't know what to think, but I do know this. The house is secure, and that's where Amanda and Jade need to be."

Amanda looked doubtful.

But it was true. I'd spent a small fortune on home security, including reinforced doors and windows and a panic room in the basement. Had I gone overboard? Probably, but fatherhood does that to a guy. You want to do everything you can to protect your family.

"Look, Amanda," I said. "Shady must have someone down there in Laredo doing his bidding." I caressed her cheek and continued, "Of that, I'm sure. The Ranger was killed only a week ago. That means Shady must have hired someone before he died, or pulled in a boatload of markers. The killer is still out there, and who knows what he plans to do next. So you need to stay here, and keep Maria close. If we need to hire extra security, we will."

"I'll stay at the house with them," Kate said.

Amanda looked at her. "Thank you, Kate. I'd appreciate that."

You probably think it's strange that my ex-lover and my wife get along so well. But what can I say? They like and respect one another.

"It's settled then," I said. "You'll stay here and be on the lookout for anything suspicious. Shady may have me over a barrel, but I'll be damned if he gets the chance to harm my family again."

Amanda held Jade just a little tighter.

We talked for a few minutes more, during which I promised I'd call my father—my attorney—as soon as I got to Texas, and that he would keep her up to date. I doubted they'd let me call her direct, but I assured her I would if I could.

Kate made arrangements to pack some things and move into one of our guest rooms. Amanda suggested Rose, my stepmother, stay with them, too. The more I thought about it, the better a private security detail sounded. In the PI business, you get to know people, and more than a few guys owed me favors. I made a mental note to ask Jacque to organize it.

As if on cue, just as Amanda left, Jacque came walking in like she owned the place, escorted by an officer, of course. Jacque is a unique woman. I've never met another one like her.

"Jacque, it's good to see you, but how the hell—"

"I talked to Chief Johnston, of course. He said I could have ten minutes, but not alone." She eyed the officer with disdain. He smiled and then ignored her.

While Kate's eyes had been wide and scared for me, and Amanda's were full of tears, Jacque's were filled with fury.

"I could kill him, Harry. I know Shady's dead already, but I could just kill him. And anyone that helped him plan this mess."

I couldn't help but smile. Jacque had been talking to Tim, apparently.

Tim was the only other person that knew what Shady had said to me during those last few moments before he died.

"You put it together, then, too, did you?" I said.

"They said you killed someone down in Laredo. It wasn't hard to figure out dat Shady was the only one we know of with a grudge against you that spent time down there, and recently, too. It has to be him. He must have planned all this before he bombed the office last month."

For a split second, a new emotion flashed across Jacque's face. Was it fear? She no doubt was thinking about her own kidnapping by Shady and his goons only a month earlier.

Jacque still hadn't told me everything that had happened those two days when he had her. She always just shrugged it off as no big deal, but I knew that Shady had scared her.

"Jacque, I think you're right. I think it was Shady who set this up before he died. I don't know how he did it or who's helping him, but we have to find out."

"We're already on it," she said. "We'll get'im, whoever it is."

I nodded. "Jacque, I'm not asking anyone to go to Texas. It could be dangerous. But I'll pay for flights and expenses and equipment and everything else if anyone does decide to go."

"Oh, we're going, all right, never you fear. Tim and TJ are already on board. Your father has put the Gulfstream at our disposal. We're flying out tonight, and I've rented a house we'll use as a remote tactical office."

I let out a long breath. I wouldn't have expected any less from my team—my friends—but it was still nice to hear.

Jacque reached up and grabbed my shoulder. "We got your back, Harry. Always."

"Thank you, Jacque."

I took the final few minutes the Chief had allowed her to bring her up to speed with what I knew so far. It wasn't much, and I certainly couldn't give her any details. I told her about the dead Texas Ranger—Cory Sloan—the gun that was supposedly registered to me, as well as my prints and DNA. I also told her about the flights and rental car I'd supposedly booked. I even threw in the previous shooting the gun was somehow tied to.

She took notes in a small notepad and nodded when I paused.

"There's one more thing, Jacque," I said, then told her about the security footage and my doppelganger. I was certain someone must have tampered with the footage. But how and when? I had no idea. Was it done before the police got hold of it? Or was there someone inside the Laredo police or Texas Rangers on Shady's payroll?

"We need to know where, when and how Shady got my gun," I said. "We need to know how my prints stayed on that gun. The person in the footage wasn't wearing gloves. I noticed that after seeing it first, so I'm sure Culp must have seen it, too."

Jacque nodded, closed her notebook and said, "We'll get right on it, Harry. Shady was thorough, but he must have made mistakes. All we have to do is find them, then his scheme will fall apart."

I nodded, but I had a feeling it wasn't going to be that easy.

"Thank you, Jacque. I really mean it. And thank Tim and TJ for me, too. I don't know what I'd do without y'all."

She left in a hurry, but before she did, I gave her verbal authorization to spend whatever was necessary, and I gave her the names of a couple of private security companies and instructions to hire one of them to watch my house. Jacque assured me she'd take care of it.

Finally, I found myself alone in my cell, alone with my thoughts.

My family was safe. My father was tracking down the best criminal defense lawyer in the state of Texas. And my team was relocating to Laredo to begin pulling apart Shady's little coup. And then I remembered the smirk on his face, just before he put the gun in his mouth and pulled the trigger. Now I knew why. He was certain he'd beaten me, even from the grave.

But he was wrong. Dead wrong.

Friday, July 18, 2019

6:30 am

T hat night in the lockup wasn't easy. I didn't sleep much. My confidence in my family's safety, in our ability to defeat this crazy trap... it all started to melt away. They say the mind is a beautiful thing, and it is, but it can be a terrible thing, too. It has a habit of churning things over and over, morphing, inventing, until a mundane situation turns into a nightmare. My situation, though, was way more than mundane, so you can imagine what my active imagination did with it.

As the night wore on, the police department grew quiet, but I couldn't sleep. I paced the cell like a captured cockroach.

If you've read any of my previous adventures, you know I'm a man of action. I move around. I prowl the streets. I go out for drinks. I like to cook for Amanda. I play golf. I go for runs. And, at work, I don't investigate from behind a desk. I hit the streets. And, often enough to be called a habit, I get myself into trouble. But the truth is, I wouldn't have it any other way. It's who I am, and I'm not going to start apologizing for it now.

So being stuck in a cell, feeling as useless as a paperweight, when there was a case to work, a puzzle to solve, a bad guy to beat... well, let's just say it was a few degrees on the wrong side of infuriating. This was especially true considering the fact that I was dealing with the most important case of my life, literally, because my life was on the line.

Finally, more out of frustration than anything else, I dropped down on the bed and fell into a shallow, infinitely disturbed sleep... for a couple of hours, maybe.

Before I knew it, Captain David Culp and his partner arrived with a police officer in tow who opened the cell door.

"We got a long drive ahead of us," Culp said. "So get yourself up and let's get this show on the road."

"No shower?" I asked. "No breakfast? Is this how you do things in Texas?"

"He said get moving, smart ass," Booth snarled.

Culp cut him a sharp look, but Booth ignored it.

I was taken to a transport van, where I was handcuffed to a chain that led to an anchor in the floor. The bench I had to sit on was cushioned, but a plank of wood would have been more comfortable. And then, we were off, heading west on I-24 toward Nashville. I didn't get to call my wife, see my father or Kate. I was alone with these two Texas Rangers, with nothing but a long day of riding to look forward to.

Well, at least I'll have some time to think.

The pitiful amount of sleep I'd gotten in the cell did help me to reset, to see things from a different perspective. And I had some questions to chew on.

How the hell did Shady get ahold of my gun?

That was the first puzzle I had to deal with. At first, I thought that maybe Shady or one of his men had snatched a gun from my office when they planted the bomb and kidnapped Jacque.

But wouldn't we have noticed that on the security footage? I thought so. Especially since Tim had the backed-up video from the security cameras right up until the explosion had cut it off. Still... it was possible, I supposed.

But then I remembered the previous killing, a drug-related multiple execution Culp had called it. So if the gun was involved in those murders, that means Shady had the gun at least a month earlier.

I shook my head. That didn't make any sense, did it? Shady would have only started working on this plan after the failed nuclear attack, when TJ and I removed his finger. It wasn't exactly the highlight of my career, I admit. But we had to get the information out of him somehow. Thousands of lives were at stake, after all.

Okay, so there were too many questions down that road. I needed Tim and TJ to work on it. If I knew them, though, they were already working on it.

How did they tamper with the security footage?

That was another question to which there was no

easy answer. The police would have gotten the footage from the Denny's system within minutes of their arrival at the scene, so how the hell could someone have doctored it? Tim would know, but it seemed like movie magic to me. To do a proper job and make it believable would have taken hours... And it looked perfect to me.

If it had been doctored, it had to have been done while it was in police custody. Did Shady have an inside man, someone in the Texas Rangers or the Laredo Police Department? Could they have switched the footage somehow? That seemed more likely.

For a moment, I hoped the inside man was John Booth. I wanted to punch his overly blue lights out. Something about him just bugged the hell out of me.

But what about the fingerprints on the gun?

If the gun was indeed mine, that is, something Jacque could easily confirm. Any forensic team worth their salt would know if the registration numbers had been tampered with.

But, assuming the gun was mine and the fingerprints were legit... how did they stay on the gun so perfectly? Maybe the shooter was wearing a glove of some sort, something thin and skin-colored, so it didn't show up in the video footage?

I frowned. It was possible. Hell, anything was possible.

Or what if the prints were planted? If there was a crooked cop involved, that would have been easy to do.

The same questions rolled around in my head again and again for what felt like hours.

In the front of the van, "One Number Away" by

Luke Combs played on the radio at least once every half hour.

Finally, the van pulled in for gas.

Culp let me out to use the restroom, under his watchful eye, of course. He even bought me a bottle of natural spring water and a large hot dog at the convenience store. It tasted like crap, but beggars can't be choosers, can they? And since I hadn't eaten since the day before, I was grateful to get anything at all.

When we headed back to the van, I took note of John Booth's hand resting annoyingly on the grip of his gun as if he was just hoping I'd give him an excuse to gun me down in the parking lot. I smiled to myself. I'd met so many just like him. Wannabe tough guys. Bad Boys, Bad Boys... Yeah, that was Booth. *Idiot!*

I glanced around the parking lot, trying to get my bearings. Where the hell were we? Arkansas, maybe?

People at the gas pumps watched us as we walked back to the van, eyeing me like I was some deranged killer. Which, of course, officially, was exactly what I was.

That's when I noticed it. An SUV. Dark blue. A Nissan Pathfinder.

It was parked at the other end of the gas station lot, with one person inside behind the wheel. The man stared at me. The face was familiar, very familiar indeed.

I didn't look too hard. I didn't want Culp or Booth to catch on and take an interest in the SUV, too, but I managed to sneak one final good look at him before I climbed clumsily into the van while trying not to drop my hot dog.

I knew who he was, and to say I was surprised to see

him of all people would be the understatement of the century.

In fact, after the doors closed and Culp started the engine, I began to doubt my sanity.

Is my mind playing tricks on me? It has to be. What the hell is he doing here? Is he following me? Is he watching over me, waiting for the right moment to step in and help?

The driver of that SUV, whom I was sure was maintaining his distance, staying a few vehicles behind, putting his CIA training to good use, was someone I knew well, really well.

Bob Ryan.

7

Friday, July 18, 2019

I remembered the first time I met Bob Ryan; he got me out of a scrape, probably saved my life.

That was years ago, just after I left the force and started my own company back in 2008. He was, had been, one of the original members of my team. I'd even made him a partner in my business, along with Jacque. Over the years he'd saved my skin at least a half-dozen times. But that all ended more than a year ago when he left me to return to the CIA.

I never did find out why he came to work for me. What I do know is that he was always CIA, even when he was working for me, though I didn't know it at the time. He revealed it the day he left. It was a shock, to be sure, and I was angry he'd never mentioned it, though I completely understood why he hadn't. When he left, he also left a large hole in my team. Bob was very much my right-hand man, my partner in just about every case I worked.

I missed the guy, and I'm not ashamed to admit it. And now, when I needed help the most, there he was.

How did he know I was in trouble? There was no way of knowing. My name couldn't have hit the press yet. That I knew because Chief Johnston had ordered his people to keep a lid on the news of my arrest. Then again, there were too many cops, including Henry Finkle, who could have leaked it... But even if someone had leaked the news, it couldn't have been more than twenty-four hours ago, so how did Bob Ryan find out?

Then again, why was I surprised? Bob had connections. And I'm not just talking about the CIA. He'd made a lot of friends while he was working for me. All it would have taken was for one of them to make a quick phone call. Hell, he and Kate had even dated for a while. Was it such a stretch that she still had a way of contacting him? Or TJ? Or Tim?

No, it wasn't a stretch at all, and the more I thought about it, the more likely it became that it was one of them.

It was just after eight that evening when we stopped again, somewhere outside of Austin, Texas. We'd been on the road for almost fourteen hours—we picked up an hour when we changed time zones—and I was a mess. The hard seat, the lack of windows, the noise... it was worse than the cell back at the PD.

This time, though, it was different. We had some decent food. Culp took off the cuffs and led me into a Cracker Barrel, saying that Booth would, and I quote, "Blow you away if you even think about running." Booth just nodded, his hand resting snuggly on the grip of his gun.

So I behaved myself. I ate some chicken fried steak, mashed potatoes and green beans, and drank two full glasses of lemonade. I was so grateful I even offered to pay if Culp would just fish my wallet out of the evidence bag in the van. He declined, of course.

Getting to Laredo was taking longer than I'd thought. Probably because the governor on the van prevented it from going any faster than seventy miles an hour.

"I take it we're not stopping anywhere for the night?" I asked Culp as we walked out of the dining room and back to the van.

"Nope. We're less than four hours out of Laredo," he replied. "We'll be in a little after midnight."

I spotted Bob Ryan browsing the books in the gift shop near the entrance. He watched us leave, peering over his sunglasses as I did my best to ignore him. I couldn't risk giving him away.

His blue SUV was parked a handful of spaces away from the big, black transport van. If the Texas Rangers hadn't noticed they were being tailed all day, then they'd never figure it out now. It would be dark soon.

The next several hours in that damn van were the hardest. I'd loaded myself with carbs, so you can imagine how sleepy I was. But, handcuffed to that uncomfortable bench, I couldn't exactly sleep. All I could do was doze a little.

I wondered where the hell we were. I didn't even know what time it was. I knew it was close to eight-thirty when we left the Cracker Barrel, but I didn't have my watch or phone, and there wasn't a clock in the van. The noise was mind-numbing. I couldn't believe I would be glad when we reached our destination, Laredo, but anything was better than that coffin of a van.

Laredo, Texas? The only thing I knew about it was the sleepy little border town in the song. I soon learned that it wasn't so little anymore, that it was one of the border towns right at the bottom of Texas, separated from Mexico and its sister city, Nuevo Laredo, by the Rio Grande.

I knew my father would already be there by the time we arrived, probably accompanied by a high-powered Texas attorney, maybe even an entire team of hotshots. I also knew that Jacque and the rest of my team would already be set up somewhere in town. The ride must have been getting to me because I began to fantasize that someone, either August or my team, had already cracked the case, and tomorrow morning they'd present their evidence, and I'd be free to go.

Of course, it was all wishful thinking, and I knew it. August had warned me that it was going to be a long and drawn-out process, and I had to prepare myself for a long and excruciating trial.

Flashes of light filled the van's windshield, visible only through a small metal grill in the reinforced bulkhead that divided the front and back compartments of the vehicle. I leaned forward to see what was going on.

More flashes, and shouting echoed through the grill and the walls.

"Can we get a picture of Harry Starke?" someone yelled.

"How sure are you that you have your man?"

"Why did you drive from Tennessee instead of flying, sir?"

The questions came streaming in. The Texas Rangers ignored them all.

It was the press. *At this time of night? I can't believe it.*

Kate and Johnston had promised there'd be zero leaks in Chattanooga, but I should have known that Texas was a different story.

The van came to a stop and Culp opened the back doors, uncuffed me and helped me out. Booth stood between us and the massive crowd of reporters that was being held back by a dozen or so uniformed police officers. We were outside a large, low building, labeled with bold black letters: Laredo Police Department.

Culp and Booth took my arms and hustled me inside. They did their best, but I had no doubt that there would be some juicy pictures in the papers and on the news the following morning.

"My how the mighty have fallen," Booth said sarcastically, once we were inside.

"How do you mean?" I asked. But to be honest, I was too damn tired to care.

"You're Harry Starke, the 'Hero of Chattanooga,'" Booth said with a sneer. "Isn't that what they were calling you just a few weeks ago?"

"Yeah, I guess."

"Well, you want to know what they're calling you here? They're calling you 'The Butcher of Laredo.' How do you feel about that?"

I honestly didn't care. I just wanted to lie down and get some sleep, and I told Booth as much, but I was sure there was nothing I could have said that would have wiped that stupid smirk off his face. He'd won, at least as far as he was concerned.

I was checked in, processed, and then led by a couple of Laredo police officers to a cell in the back of the building... Well, not exactly a cell, more a large cage, one of three set against a wall of a much larger room with several tables and chairs. I was the only occupant.

Several other cops were standing along the path, staring me down. Not a one of them had a look that said anything other than murder.

I was sure that, if the power had gone out and the security cameras had been turned off, these cops would have beaten me to death without a second thought.

And why not? To them, I was a cop killer. I'd gunned down one of their own in cold blood. Everyone there had seen the security footage. Of that, I was sure.

I didn't blame them for feeling the way they did. I was so exhausted from the drive that I didn't even care how roughly the cops shoved me into the cage and slammed the door shut behind me.

Finally, I was left alone, except for a single guard who played something on his phone half the night... and I didn't care.

I kicked off my shoes, wished I could have a shower and a change of clothes, two things I quickly forgot about once I stretched out on the hard bunk in the corner.

I'd been falsely arrested for killing a cop.

I'd been driven halfway across the country.

Half the state of Texas wanted me dead.

But at that moment. I didn't care.

I fell asleep thinking of Amanda. Her smile. Her laugh. And Jade's shining eyes when she looked up at me, her eyes full of love. Full of love...

8

Saturday, July 19, 2019

Morning

I slept like a rock that night. The next morning, I was taken to the showers where two police officers watched me as if I was a rabid dog they wanted to put down. I didn't mind though. I was just happy to get a shower and a change of clothes. The clothes happened to be a gray jumpsuit and matching slippers. A size too big even for my body type, but that just meant I had plenty of room to move around.

I'd been back in my little cage for all of fifteen minutes when an officer came and took me to a small interrogation room. There was no camera in this one, though, just a table and four chairs. Seated on one of those chairs was my father, and boy did he ever look tired. The tiny wrinkles around his eyes were deeper than ever, but he was dressed smartly, and he had a stack of papers in front of him.

Seated next to my father was a man I hadn't seen before. He was dressed in an expensive, dark gray suit, white shirt and blue tie. I guessed right away who he was, and I was right.

"My name is Raymundo Ortiz," he said, rising to his feet and offering me his hand. "I'm a defense lawyer and, with your permission, I would like to represent you." His handshake was strong. Confident.

I nodded. "Well, if my father recommends you, I'd be dumb not to accept your help, Mr. Ortiz."

We all sat down. August looked me over and said, "How are you, Harry?"

"I've been better," I replied. "Everyone here would like to kill me, but they've been professional so far."

Ortiz nodded sharply. "Good. I have something for you that will help, I think."

He reached down and took a takeaway box from a briefcase on the floor beside his chair. He also produced a huge to-go cup of the hottest, strongest coffee I'd ever tasted. It was marvelous.

The food was good, too. Breakfast burritos, hash, and refried beans. The box said *Taco Palenque* on the cover. I'd never heard of such a place, but the food was first-rate.

"Mr. Ortiz is from a firm in Austin," my father said. "He's the best in the state."

Raymundo Ortiz didn't deny it. "My team is working on your case as we speak, Harry. Is it all right that I call you Harry?"

"Of course," I said. "My team's on it, too, Mr. Ortiz."

The attorney frowned. "I'm sorry, I don't follow."

"You mean from your agency?" August asked. "They're here, in Laredo?"

"That's right," I said, nodded at my father, then took a sip of my coffee. I turned to Mr. Ortiz. "But my father has suggested our two teams shouldn't share information."

Ortiz nodded. "I would agree wholeheartedly, Harry. We don't want to do anything that could contaminate our defense. As you have already noticed, you are not exactly the most popular person in this town. The DA and the Judge will both be wanting to see you executed, and it is probable that the jury will want the same thing. I am afraid the cards are very much stacked against you."

I put down my fork. The word "execution" has a way of crushing a man's appetite.

"Yes, I'm sure they are," I said dryly.

He nodded and continued, "Your father filled me in yesterday. Unfortunately, we don't have full access to the evidence they have against you, and we won't until after the arraignment. What we have are summary files only."

"Okay, fine." I sighed. "I've been thinking. We need to figure out how someone got hold of my gun. And how the fingerprints were planted. Oh, and the security footage. It must have been tampered with. I thought about it a lot on the way down here. The only thing I can think of is that someone in the police department switched the footage after it was taken into evidence. That would mean there was an inside man, or woman, involved."

Ortiz raised a hand, his brown eyes boring into me,

and said, "I think we should take a step back from that, Harry. It wouldn't be prudent to talk about crooked cops right now. It would not be helpful. As it is, every cop in Texas wants you dead right now, remember?"

I felt my face get hot. I didn't like it, but, on thinking about it for a moment, I realized Ortiz was probably right.

"So, let's begin with something a little more basic," Raymundo continued. "We have your alibi for Sloan's murder. I'll be reaching out to your wife and babysitter, of course."

I nodded.

"Good. But we have yet to establish an alibi for the day of the other murders." Ortiz gave me the date. "We really need to know your whereabouts on that day, Harry."

I leaned back in my chair. "Are you kidding? Everyone in Chattanooga knows what I was doing that day. I was saving the city from a nuclear attack."

"The Hero of Chattanooga, is that right?"

"Well, I don't call myself that, but yeah."

"Okay, so it would have been impossible for you to fly down to Texas and kill someone?"

I raised my hands. Was this guy serious?

"You were not on a plane that day. You will swear to that in court?"

It was at that moment I began to feel dizzy. It was almost surreal. What did Raymundo Ortiz know?

Because, yes, I was on a plane that day. I was on a plane flying over a boiling lake, kicking Duvon James's body into the water to be dissolved into nothing.

I made sure to speak slowly, careful with my words.

"I'm not sure exactly what you're asking, Mr. Ortiz. Can you spell it out for me?"

The lawyer cocked his head to one side. "It is a simple question, Harry. Did you fly down to Texas that day? That is what the prosecutor will ask you, and you are not doing a very good job of answering that question. Right now, it is just the three of us in a room together. How will you do in front of a judge and jury?"

I glanced at my father. He was staring at me, too. What was he thinking? Was I starting to look guilty to him, too?

"Look," I said. "I did not fly to Texas that day... You're barking up the wrong tree here. And I mean it when I say tree. Because Lester Shady Tree is behind this mess. He framed me, somehow. We just need to figure out how, and we won't have to worry about this ever going to trial."

Ortiz looked down at his notes, uncomfortable for a moment. "Yes, your father did share with me your theory of a criminal nemesis framing you from beyond the grave. I promise I have people looking into that. But I have to say. It does not look promising."

"How the hell do you know?" I didn't mean to raise my voice, really. But this guy was making me angry.

I got up from my chair. "Look. If my father says you're the best, then I believe him. But if you don't figure out what Shady did, then you won't be able to help me. Period. I don't care how unpromising it sounds."

I turned toward the door.

"Son," August said, his voice quiet but sharp, charged with a quiet fury. "You need to sit down and—"

"No," I cut him off. "You keep working on this. But

I'm going to see if I can call my wife and Jacque and see what my team has found. Get back to me when you have something that can get me out of here."

I knocked on the door. A cop opened it immediately and, without saying a word, took me back to my cage.

The department was full of cops during the daytime, and they all stared at me. I was sure they were mentally slitting my throat, but I was too angry to care.

Not at my father. Not even at Ortiz. He was just doing his job, and he was right. The whole damn thing was far-fetched. But Ortiz didn't know Shady. I did. And I knew he was behind it. The only question now was how the hell was I going to get myself out of it?

9

Saturday, July 19, 2019

Morning

A half an hour later, back in my cage, I was still seething.

A police officer, an unusually tall woman, her hands on her belt like a sheriff might stand in an old western movie, was watching me from the other side of the room. She was giving me the evil eye. I ignored her.

As I sat on my cot and stewed, something Jacque had said came back to me. "Shady made mistakes." And I knew from experience she was right, that he did make mistakes. His plan was good, too damn good, but somewhere along the line he'd messed up, had to have.

And it wasn't just about getting me out of jail, either. Shady had planned for a Texas Ranger to be murdered in cold blood in order to frame me. That meant that, while I was sitting in that cage receiving nasty looks from every cop in the building, the real killer was out there walking free.

That needed to change, and quickly.

The door at the far end of the room opened, and a police officer came in, escorting two people I'd never expected to see.

I stood up from my bunk, shocked.

"Amanda, Jacque? What are you doing here?"

Amanda walked right up to the bars, looking at me with determination, Jacque right behind her, a bemused smile on her face.

Amanda raised an eyebrow. "You didn't think for one minute that I was going to stay in Chattanooga, did you?"

"I thought I told you to stay safe."

"Oh, sure, in the one place Shady's cohorts would know to look, right? Our home. I don't think so, Tiger."

I shook my head, then I looked at Jacque.

"Were you behind this, Jacque, and how come they let the both of you in anyway?"

"You can thank Captain Culp for that—"

Before she could say more, the female officer stalked across the room, opened my cage door and pointed to one of the tables.

"You have thirty minutes. No touching."

"Oh, don't look at me like that, Harry," Jacque said as we sat down at the table. "This was all Kate and Amanda's doing. But they're right, you know. Your house is the least safe place in the universe right now. I have a security company watching it, just in case... and that makes it a good decoy. Only for now though, but Amanda's safe here with us. Jade too."

They were right, of course. Staying behind in Chattanooga was just asking to be attacked or kidnapped. And who knew what else Shady had up his sleeve?

It was still hard to believe that he was dead. And yet he was still finding new ways to ruin our lives.

"You better be glad Amanda came along, too," Jacque added. "I don't think they would have let me back here without her, even with Culp's say-so. It's family visitors only for the Butcher of Laredo."

My mouth fell open. "Now where did you hear that?"

Jacque held up a newspaper. It was a copy of the Laredo Morning Times. And, not surprisingly, my picture was on the front page. The headline called me The Butcher of Laredo.

I shook my head. "I think I know who came up with that." It was sad to think that John Booth had been talking to the press.

"I have someone who wants to speak with you," Jacque said, holding up a phone.

I looked around at the tall officer. She glared at me but nodded her head.

I returned her nod, then said, "Put it on speaker, Jacque."

I thought it might have been my father, still unhappy with the way I walked out on him and Ortiz, but it wasn't.

"Hey, Mr. Starke."

"Tim? Is that you?"

Boy was I glad to hear from him. I hadn't had the chance to talk to him since before we left for the cabin.

"We're all set up, Harry," he said. "I have some new computers. Jacque said it was okay."

"Absolutely. Just tell me what you know so far."

"Okay, but don't be mad at me. I have some... information, stuff that isn't available publicly, if you catch my drift."

I glanced again at the tall policewoman. She was distracted, doing something on her phone, but I didn't want to take any chances.

I leaned forward and said in a low voice, "Tim, be careful what you say. I'm in a police station and you're on speaker."

"Right... right. So I'll just, uh, cut to the chase. We know the serial number of the murder weapon. It is registered to you."

I nodded. "I figured as much. Go on."

"You purchased it legally and you are licensed to carry it, which is a good thing."

"Of course," I said, a bit defensively. "That's the only way I buy a gun. You know that."

"Right, of course." Tim started speaking a bit faster. "What I mean is we can prove when and where you bought the gun. We have receipts and everything. All digitized, so even the bomb didn't remove that evidence."

"And?" I was becoming impatient.

"You bought that particular gun after the nuclear incident, Harry."

Tim paused, letting that sink in.

"You mean, we can prove I didn't have anything to do with that previous multiple-victim execution?"

Jacque jumped in. "Well, we can prove that your gun wasn't there."

"Yeah," Tim added. "And that kind of puts into question all the other evidence against you, right?"

"You bet it does," I said. "This is great news, Tim."

"So here's what I'm thinking," Tim continued. "Shady or somebody somehow got hold of your gun and brought it down to Texas. It really was this gun, your gun, that killed that Texas Ranger, okay? But then—and I don't know this for sure yet because I haven't hack... I mean I haven't looked into the ballistics reports. I think someone altered the digital evidence files for the shooting a few months ago so it would match your gun, too. I know if you gave me fifteen minutes with those files, I could prove they were fake. And if I could do it..."

He trailed off, but I was right there to pick up the line of thought.

"If you could do it," I said, "then the technicians that work with the Texas Rangers, or even the FBI, could prove it, too."

"Exactly," Tim said. "And that sets the whole case on fire."

Amanda was shaking her head. "I don't get it. They still have all this evidence against you for the more recent killing. And Tim just said that doesn't seem to be fake."

"All this evidence," I said, "this framing job Shady planned for me, it's like a house of cards. Once one card falls, everything else becomes suspect."

Amanda, obviously thinking things through, nodded.

"And all you need is reasonable doubt and they don't get a conviction. In fact, I'll bet the prosecutor won't even take it to trial."

"Plus," Jacque added, "those Texas Rangers will realize they don't have the right man. They'll start looking at the evidence from a completely different perspective."

I smiled, thinking, my mind in a whirl.

"That's it then, I guess," Tim said excitedly over the phone. "I just have to get this to your attorney and he'll get you off the hook, right?"

I heaved a sigh and said, "No, Tim. That won't work."

"Why not?" The kid sounded hurt.

"Well, for starters, you work for me, so you can't be the one to deliver the evidence. My new criminal defense lawyer said that would be a bad idea. Plus, you obtained some of that evidence via less than ethical means. I need Ortiz to obtain it somehow himself."

Amanda and Jacque both nodded in unison, but it was Amanda that spoke up. "That makes sense, Harry, but there's nothing to stop you from pointing him in the right direction, is there? Then the digital tampering can be exposed legitimately?"

I stared at Jacque. Something else was bothering me, but I couldn't put my finger on what it was. I decided to work through it out loud.

"Okay, so Shady was sure this would sink me for good. He was so confident up on that catwalk that day, just before he... just before he died."

They both nodded, but they didn't interrupt.

"Shady was smart, very smart, so he must have known that all his evidence would fall apart under careful scrutiny."

"So what are you thinking, then, Harry?" Tim said.

I pursed my lips, shaking my head, wishing I had a good answer, but the truth was I really wasn't sure what I was thinking.

"I don't know what Shady had planned," I said, "but there's so much evidence stacked against me. Not just my gun, but my prints and DNA and my face on the security footage. Not just one murder, but several. Not just anybody killed, but a Texas Ranger."

Jacque nodded and said, "Yes, and all the details that came up all at once. The flights that were booked. The car rental. It's... overwhelming."

"It is," I agreed. "I think there's something else going on here. It's almost as if all the evidence was put in place to make sure I was brought down here to Texas as quickly as possible."

Amanda's eyes grew wide. "But why? Why would he want you here?"

"My question exactly," I replied thoughtfully.

We were all quiet for a minute. The thought of another shoe about to drop wasn't a comfortable one.

You see, normally, when I know something's coming, I can prepare for it.

But this was different. I had no idea where the next attack would come from, and there was nothing I could do to prepare for it.

"There's something else, Mr. Starke," Tim said, his voice cracking a bit over the phone connection. "I... well, let's just say I took a peek at the security footage from the Denny's."

I glanced over at the cop across the room once again. She was talking on the phone.

"Go on," I said.

"Well, I guess you assumed the same thing I did, that the footage had been altered to include your face."

"That's right. I did. What did you find, Tim?"

This was another key. If we could show that the footage had been altered, we could prove that I was being framed. And maybe, just maybe, if we moved fast enough, I could be released from custody before the rest of Shady's plan could be executed.

"Well, I don't know what it means, exactly," Tim said, "but the footage is legit."

I was stunned. "What? You mean—"

"I mean there's someone out there that looks exactly like you. The killer really is your doppelganger."

"Wow," Amanda said. "That's freaky. How did they do that? How did they find someone that looked just like you?"

"Plastic surgery, no doubt," Jacque said.

That was too much of a stretch, even for Shady. It was the stuff of fantasy, a movie script.

"I don't think so," I said. "Shady got lucky, is all."

"Time's up, folks," the female officer said, putting away her phone.

"We have to go, Tim," I said. "Thanks for all you're doing. Just keep digging. Maybe something will come up."

He promised he would, told me that TJ was looking

into other angles, and then he hung up. Jacque excused herself, leaving me alone with Amanda.

I reached across the table and took her hand.

"No touching."

I turned to look at the woman, my eyes pleading. She nodded once and then looked away.

"Be careful, Harry," Amanda whispered. "If something else is coming, you have to be ready for it."

I promised her I would, squeezed her hand and two minutes later, she was gone and I was back in my cage and on my cot, staring up at the ceiling.

I now knew that the evidence against me wouldn't hold up. I also knew that that wouldn't be the end of it. I hated to admit it, but the ball was now in Shady's court, and all I could do was wait.

10

Saturday, July 19, 2019

Afternoon

The afternoon passed slowly. I'd hoped that maybe my father would visit, or maybe Ortiz, but they didn't, and that was fine. I knew everyone was doing all they could. My job was to sit tight... Hell, it wasn't as if I had a choice.

So, I took advantage of the free time to do some floor exercises. Is it cliché to do pushups in a jail cell? Sure. Did I care? Hell no. I needed to stay fit, sharp and focused and, as Amanda had said, I needed to be ready for whatever Shady had planned for me next.

Evening came and a cop brought me a hamburger, fries, a cup of coffee and a bottle of water. It was all I'd had since the breakfast burrito that Ortiz had brought me that morning, and I'm ashamed to say I inhaled it.

As I lay there on my cot, eyes closed, hands behind my head, I continued to mull over everything I knew about the case. While shuffling facts and images around in my head, I kept coming back to the guy that looked like me. How did Shady manage that? It was perfect. The guy could have been my identical twin. Had I not known better, I would have said it was me.

I smiled to myself when I remembered the look on August's face when he saw the footage. I could tell that he was bamboozled too.

None of it made sense. It was as if Shady was playing with me... and I suppose he was.

The main lights were shut off. Every third light in the ceiling stayed on, giving the police department—what I could see of it—an eerie feel. I figured there was only a skeleton crew on duty.

As I lay there in the semi-darkness, my brain began to play tricks on me. My imagination ran wild. If anything was going to happen, right then would have been a good time. If Shady had hired someone to kill or kidnap me, it was the perfect time to do it, when security would be minimal.

And that's probably why I jumped up off the cot when the door opened. A guy wearing jeans and a black tee under a tan leather jacket walked in and came right up to my cage.

"Harry Starke?" he asked, as he pulled back his jacket to reveal a gold badge and weapon on his belt.

He looked to be about my age, black, with a shaved head and sharp, angry eyes.

This is it, I guess. This cop, or thug disguised as a cop, is going to gun me down. I'll die as The Butcher of Laredo.

I walked over and faced him through the bars.

"Yes?"

To my surprise and delight, he didn't pull the weapon. Instead, he stood there silently for a moment, eyeing me up and down slowly with those dark, intensely sharp and angry eyes.

"Can I help you?" I said finally.

He clicked his tongue then said, or should I say, growled, "It isn't you."

"I'm sorry?"

"It isn't you," he repeated, as if that was supposed to mean anything to me. "I don't know why," he continued, "but you're being set up, Starke."

Well now, that's not what I expected.

"I'm glad to hear someone in the Laredo PD believes me. Your name is?"

"Door. Stanley Door. Lieutenant Door." He spoke loudly and sharply.

"Well, Lieutenant Door. I'm glad you don't believe I'm a cop killer."

His demeanor changed in a flash. His eyebrows twisted in anger.

"I don't know anything about who killed Sloan last week. That could have been you. Probably was, in fact. Unless you got a twin. I've seen the security tapes."

I looked at him, confused.

"I'm talking about the drug shooting a couple of months back. I know you didn't do that."

My eyebrows raised. "Oh?"

"I work with the DEA, organized crime, drug enforcement task force. We've been investigating cartel activity along the border here for more than three years. We're pretty sure we know who executed those people. I don't care what gun they're saying was used—the records are wrong. We have people already looking into it."

I nodded. "I can prove the ballistics records have been tampered with, Lieutenant."

His lips twitched. He almost smiled, but he didn't.

"Oh, really?" he said. "You can do that from lockup? Well, that is interesting."

"Well, I can't personally, but my team can. I run a private investigation agency in Chattanooga, and my people can prove I didn't even own that gun when the killings took place. In fact, they can prove hackers altered the forensic files."

"Digital files, humph." Door practically spat the words. "Supposed to be this big advancement over paper, boxes and shelves. It ain't so. Hackers can't do anything with actual physical evidence. I wouldn't call that an advancement."

It was then, in the low light, I realized I'd mistaken the cop's age. He'd looked to be about my age, maybe even a little younger, but as I squinted, I could see the tiny wrinkles around his eyes. He was older than me. Maybe as much as ten years my senior. He would remember the days of paper files and evidence boxes being front and center in an investigation.

"Those were the days," I said. "I was on the force, Chattanooga PD. I left in '08."

Door's eyes widened. "Really? I got a cousin that's a cop in Nashville. Haven't seen her in years."

"You should come on up and visit her sometime and stop by Chattanooga. I'll show you around." Yeah, I was working him. Can you blame me? I needed a friend, and Lieutenant Stanley Door seemed to be my best bet.

He raised an eyebrow and nodded. "Maybe... If they don't give you the needle for shooting that Texas Ranger, that is."

"They won't, Lieutenant," I said. "I didn't do it, and we're going to prove it."

Door seemed to chew on that for a moment. "I don't know nothing about that, like I told ya. If you are being set up, I hope you can get out of it. If you don't, you'll get the needle, for sure."

Thanks. I didn't need that ugly reminder.

"But I do know about the execution," he continued. "The cartels are fighting on the other side. That's what they call it around here, across the border. They call it the other side. *El otro lado.* Anyway, two cartels are at war, the big guys and the local boys. That war spills over to this side sometimes."

I nodded. I'd heard a thing or two about the drug cartels along the Mexican border. Who hadn't? The drugs and arms smuggling. The human trafficking. A couple of years earlier, every news outlet in the country was talking about it and the wall Trump was building. But, beyond the headlines, I didn't know much about what happened in this part of the country. We always had too much to handle in our own neck of the woods.

"You can prove it?" I finally asked. "You can prove that someone else executed those people?"

This time Door did smile. "Well, like you said, I can't prove it myself, but my team can. The DEA boys were getting places with that investigation, making connections and such. Then the Texas Rangers swooped in and took the case over because, so they claimed, you were the prime suspect. But we didn't believe it. Not even for a minute."

As you can probably imagine, I was very happy to hear it. Everyone else I'd run into so far in Laredo was strongly on team *Butcher of Laredo*. They all wanted me dead, to get the needle, as Door so eloquently put it. So yes, it was nice to hear that someone was on my side for a change, even tenuously. As I said earlier, I needed every friend I could get.

"Anyway," Door said with a shrug. "You just be careful, you heah? My fellow officers are good men and women, but they're angry. Sloan was a popular guy. You catch my drift?"

"Yes, I do," I said. "Thanks for the warning."

Door nodded.

And, just like that, without saying another word, he turned and walked out of the room.

What a strange man. Well, at least he can get me off the hook for one murder.

And that was good because I really didn't want to have to go through the events of the days surrounding the failed nuclear attack on Chattanooga. As I've said, my conscience is clear. I did what I had to do to keep the city,

and my family, safe. But I wouldn't trust a jury to neces-
sarily feel the same.

Left alone once again, I lay back on the cot, asking
myself the same question again and again, almost like a
mantra.

What's the next move, Shady?

As it turned out, I didn't have to wait long for the
answer.

11

Sunday, July 20, 2019

Early morning

I finally got to sleep at around three in the morning. At least I figured it was about three, but it was more of a guess as I had only my internal clock to go on.

I woke up every time I heard even the slightest noise. Every door that opened or closed, every officer that walked by, every voice echoing from elsewhere in the station.

It was hard work, doing nothing, waiting for the other shoe to drop.

I asked for breakfast, but none of the sneering cops were willing to get me anything. One of them finally fetched me a cup of lukewarm coffee, which I downed in large gulps, trying not to think about anyone spitting in it before handing it to me. It tasted foul, but at least it was wet, strong and caffeinated.

Thankfully, there was a small sink in the corner of my cage, so I was able to refill the cup with tap water. It tasted terrible, coppery, bitter, but I figured it would keep me hydrated, if it didn't poison me first.

I asked to make a phone call and was denied. I'd hoped August or Ortiz would visit. Or maybe even Amanda, but nobody came. *It's fine,* I kept telling myself. They were probably all working hard to get me out of there.

Finally, late that morning, two uniformed officers approached the cage.

One was the tall woman that had been present most of the day before. The man was young and muscular. He wore sunglasses inside as if he was trying to out-cool his drastically rising hairline.

"You're being moved, Starke," the man said, his voice harsh.

"Moved where?" I asked as I approached the bars.

"To the Webb County Jail. Downtown."

I stood my ground. "I want to talk to my lawyer."

The man unlocked the cage door, opened it and stepped inside.

"You'll get your phone call at the jail," he said. "You'll like the jail. You get three squares and yard time."

I didn't like it. I didn't like it at all. I didn't like the anger in this officer's voice. I didn't like the nasty look the tall woman officer was giving me, either. And I didn't like being transferred without warning, or without being allowed to talk to my attorney, but what choice did I have?

The officer—his tag identified him as J. Thorne—cuffed me and led me out of the cage.

Lieutenant Door came in from the other room. This was the first time I noticed that the older officer had a limp. An old injury?

"What do you think you're doing, Thorne?" Door said, his voice sharp as a band saw.

"He's being transferred," the tall woman officer said.

"Who authorized it?" Door's hands were in fists. What was going on?

"Take it up with the Captain," Thorne said, pulling me by my upper arm. "The paperwork's in."

Door looked at me as Thorne pulled on me, trying to get me to turn around and walk down the hall. "Remember what I said last night," he said. "You watch your back, you heah?"

I nodded and let myself be led down the hall, back out the same exit through which I'd entered two nights earlier.

Too many things to count were churning through my mind. I'd thought there was an inside man, or woman, on the force. Was this Shady's plan? Were these two officers going to take me out to a lonely road somewhere and shoot me, leaving me in a shallow grave for the coyotes?

I'd only thought there was a crooked cop involved when I was sure the security footage from the Denny's had been altered after being taken into evidence. But Tim had revealed that the footage hadn't been tampered with. That meant no crooked cop, right? I didn't know.

Perhaps the plan was to get me into the county jail so that an inmate could shank me. Again, it was a possibility.

We stepped out into blazing sunlight that temporarily blinded me. I heard an airplane flying low and figured we must have been close to the airport, the plane either taking off or landing.

Then, before I knew it, I was once again chained to a bench in the back of a van.

Couldn't they just put me in the back of a cruiser? At least that way I'd be able to see where I was going.

My mind was racing as the engine started and the van began to move.

How far away was this jail downtown? I had no idea. I was shocked to realize I had no idea how big Laredo was. It wasn't a great metropolis, surely. Maybe smaller than Chattanooga? I imagined so.

The van didn't seem to be moving very quickly. It made several turns along the way, first left, then right... I heard another plane overhead.

Then, suddenly, the van came to a screeching stop and I almost fell to the floor.

Geez. What's happening now?

I heard someone shout outside the van. I didn't understand what was said.

The male officer, Thorne, yelled something back in what sounded like a very Americanized Spanish.

One of the doors opened. The vehicle rocked as someone got out. At least, that's what I imagined was happening.

More yelling, some in Spanish, some in English.

Some cursing, and then I knew. Deep down inside, I knew what was about to happen.

I dropped off the bench, hitting my knees hard, and lay flat on the floor.

Half a second later, the first gunshot exploded, then a dozen more, along with several bursts of automatic fire.

The van was under attack.

12

Sunday, July 20, 2019

Mid-morning

I swore as the van rocked beneath me. Small arms fire, automatic fire, and quick bursts sounded out, accompanied by yelling and cursing. It couldn't have lasted more than a few seconds, then it was over, and all went quiet, deathly quiet, and I knew I had only seconds before someone would come for me.

I imagined some cartel soldier, a soldado, a tattooed face, a machine gun leveled at me, a smile before he turned me into Swiss cheese. Not happy images, I can tell you.

The lock on the rear door clicked. Then the back door of the van swung open and a young kid of about eighteen climbed inside, a pistol stuck in his waistband and a set of bolt cutters in his hands.

I tensed as the kid set the cutters to the chain between the cuffs and grunted as he applied pressure. The chain snapped. I threw myself at him. I hit him with my shoulder and he staggered backward out through the open door, banging into it as he went. The door swung shut under the impact but didn't latch.

I didn't have time to think. I leaped after him. My only hope was the element of surprise. I knew they didn't want to kill me, not then anyway. If they had, they would have shot at the van. It wasn't armored, not as far as I could tell. If they'd wanted me dead, whoever *they* were, they could have filled the vehicle full of holes before opening the door. That meant they wanted me alive. That, as far as I was concerned, was not an option.

I hit the partially open door hard with my shoulder. It was open again and slammed into something... or someone, with enough force to do damage. And then I was out in blinding sunlight, on top of the kid, swinging hard. Out of the corner of my eye, I could see someone off to the left. I needed the kid's gun. He was wiry, and I couldn't get a good punch at him. I grabbed at his belt. He was either street-smart or desperate, because he twisted violently to his right. I punched him in the head and reached for his gun.

I knew from the sounds of the attacker's weapons when they opened fire on the van that there had to be at least three of them. What I didn't expect was the person standing behind the door, just far enough to the right to not get hit when I jumped out.

I felt the cold steel of the kid's pistol in my hand. I was just a split second from pulling the trigger when something slammed into my shoulder from behind. My jaw spasmed and my teeth clamped shut. My hand flopped away from the gun and my body went rigid, out of control. I'd just been zapped with a taser.

My back and shoulders spasmed. My legs folded beneath me and I grunted as I hit the ground. The pain was... unusual, almost distant. Perhaps that was because it throbbed through my entire body instead of being localized.

I'd been tased before so I knew what it felt like, but no matter how tough you think you are, it's completely debilitating and never a pleasant experience.

I tried to turn myself over to look up at them, but I still had almost no control over my body when two new guys fell on me, grabbed my arms, and hauled me to my feet.

The guy with the taser, a large, overweight Latino wearing a bright red ball cap—no face tattoo—looked at me and smiled, flashing a mouthful of mostly gold teeth.

"You ain't so tough, hombre," he said. "They said you'd be tough, so I brought this." The fat man waved his taser at my face as he grinned.

Slowly, my body recovered until I had enough strength to stand without help, but the two guys holding me didn't let go.

There was a moan from behind the still open van door. A guy with long black hair pulled back in a braid, and wearing hoop earrings, crawled into view. The door must have hit him pretty hard.

The fat man turned to face him. Without a word, he took a step forward and kicked the guy in the ribs, once, twice. The third time, I heard something crack. I think it was his arm.

"Get up," the fat man yelled.

Ponytail sniffed and struggled to get to his feet.

Fat Man turned to the kid who I'd tackled in the van.

"You okay, boy?"

The kid nodded.

"That is good. If this *güero* had gotten that gun away from you, I'd have killed you. You know that, *si?*"

The kid kept his eyes lowered and nodded.

Ponytail was up on his feet now, his gun in his hand.

I didn't bother to struggle. I was outmanned and outgunned. Especially so when a fifth guy came around the van, an Uzi in his hand.

Sirens sounded in the distance.

Fat Man looked around. "We need to move."

They pulled me around to the front of the van. The scene there was gruesome. Officer Thorne and the tall woman were both shot to a pulp. I felt sorry for them, especially because, not five minutes ago, I had suspected one or both of them of being crooked cops. But apparently, they'd just been doing their job, and now they were dead.

I was put into the rear seat of a Jeep Patriot. One of the guys got in next to me and covered me with his gun. Fat Man climbed awkwardly into the front passenger seat, and he, too, covered me with his gun. I was screwed and I knew it.

The Patriot took off, burning rubber. A second vehicle, a Cadillac CT6, following close behind.

I could hear sirens, but I never saw a police cruiser.

My captors knew exactly which roads to take to avoid law enforcement.

I kept my eyes open, trying to memorize anything I could, street signs, landmarks, anything that might help me get my bearings.

I turned my head to glance out of the side window, just for a second, but it didn't work.

When I turned again and looked at the armed man sitting next to me, I was just in time to see him jab a syringe into my thigh and thumb the plunger.

"Night night, Hot Shot," the fat man said.

My world became fuzzy, and I knew better than to try to fight it.

I leaned my head against the window and allowed the darkness to envelop me.

13

Sunday, July 20, 2019

Early afternoon

I remember nothing else about the drive. I didn't begin to come out of it until someone dragged me bodily out of the Jeep and into a ratty old house of some kind. I couldn't tell if ten minutes had passed or ten hours and, in my drug-induced haze, I didn't much care.

When I did finally come to, I found myself on the floor in a small room devoid of furniture except for a chair in one corner. The room was dimly lit by a small window. A second door stood open, and I could see it led to a small bathroom. I was in what once had been a bedroom.

I struggled up off the floor and went into the bathroom where I found a washbasin, a toilet, and a small shower complete with a mildewed plastic curtain: no soap, no towels, just a half-used roll of toilet paper.

There was a small window in the shower, too small to climb out of, even if it hadn't been nailed shut. And there was nothing in the bathroom or the bedroom I could use as a weapon, unless I planned to fight my way out with the roll of toilet paper.

I returned to the bedroom and looked out of the window. It, too, had been nailed shut, but overlooked a backyard encircled by a wooden fence where two men were seated near a smoking grill. One of them noticed me peeking out the window and waved, a big smile on his face. The other was Ponytail, still clutching his arm. Both of them were armed.

The bedroom door opened. I turned around to see Fat Man standing in the doorway with a can of beer in his hand. He stepped into the room and offered me the beer. I took it gratefully, popped the top and took a deep swallow. I don't think anything ever tasted so good.

"We got a couple of hours until we move again," he said. "Don't worry, my friend. I will bring you some brisket when it is cooked, maybe in twenty minutes."

Now you can probably understand why I was puzzled by how friendly he was. He could see that I was and raised his hands. "Look, Hot Shot, we got no beef with you. We just following orders, you know? You used to be a cop, right? So you know what I'm talking about."

"How did you know that?" I asked, hoping to keep him talking and maybe get a handle on what was coming next.

"Bro, your picture is all over the news an' stuff."

Did he just call me bro?

"Okay, so don't you try anything. You see the

cameras, right?" He jerked his head up and pointed to the corner of the room.

No, I hadn't noticed the cameras, but I did then. There were two small webcams mounted on the wall in opposite corners.

"We're watching. Just sit tight. Don't make us hurt you an' we won't."

Fat Man turned to walk out of the room.

"Wait," I said. "What happens in a couple of hours?"

The big guy turned back, one eyebrow raised. "You really don't know?" He shook his head. "I ain't got no clue how you ended up in the middle of this, Hot Shot but, then again, I don't care. You're going across to the other side."

"Why would you take me to Mexico?" I needed something, anything, to help me figure out what was happening.

Fat Man smiled, showing his golden teeth. "You're going to meet the Carbenas, white boy. What they do with you ain't none o' my business."

He smiled, turned away and left the room, bolting the door on the outside, twice. There was no way I could kick my way through that, not without alerting my captors.

The Carbenas? Now, that's a name I've heard before.

Named for the Carbena family, the cartel had been given a lot of publicity in the media over the last several years. Apparently, they were about as scary as they come.

It made sense that Shady would attach himself to the worst of the worst. So was this his plan? Get me across into Mexico so I could be tortured and killed?

I have to say, I really didn't find the idea too appealing.

I shook my head at the thought, wondering how the hell I was going to get myself out of this new mess. Nothing came readily to mind, so I decided to ignore the cameras and take a look around. I checked every corner, every floorboard, and every square inch of the bathroom, too.

I looked out of the window and could see that Ponytail and his companion were watching me on a laptop like a couple of hawks. Even if I'd managed to open a window and jump through, they'd be on me before my feet touched the ground.

I didn't even know where I was... Somewhere in Laredo, I assumed. The sun was still high in the sky, which meant I hadn't been unconscious for more than an hour or two.

I wondered what the police were doing. *Surely they must be hunting for me*, I thought. The chances of them finding me? I figured they were slim to none.

I could imagine the headlines now: *Butcher of Laredo Escapes with Cartel Help*.

Finally, I gave up and sat down on the chair and sipped what was left of the beer. What else could I do?

A few minutes later I heard the bolts on the outside of the door being drawn. The door opened and two men stepped inside, one with a pistol, which he pointed at me, the other holding a plate of smoked brisket, beans, potato salad, and a plastic knife and fork.

The second I saw the food, I remembered how

hungry I was. I thanked the two thugs. They both nodded and then left, bolting the door as they went.

I nodded up at the cameras to thank the fat guy, who I assumed was in charge, and then I sat down to eat.

The meat was... amazing, slow-cooked, tender, and there was plenty of it. The meal was so good I almost forgot I'd been kidnapped and was about to be turned over to one of the Mexican cartels.

It must have been about an hour later when Fat Man returned.

"Time to go, Hot Shot," he said. "No funny business an' you can get delivered with all your fingers intact."

I grimaced at the thought. Did he know that's what we'd done to Shady? Or was the talk of losing my fingers just a coincidence? I wasn't about to ask him.

He cuffed my hands behind my back, and then I was put into the back seat of the Jeep with a black bag put over my head. So much for trying to memorize landmarks.

The drive seemed longer than it probably was, but finally the Jeep pulled over and came to a stop.

The door opened and someone grabbed my arm and hauled me roughly out of the vehicle, then took the bag off my head.

I squinted in the light of the last rays of the sun. We were on the bank of a river. The Rio Grande, I imagined. The blue sky was slowly darkening and turning red. I looked across the river and could see a group of men, a half-dozen trucks and SUVs and a small flatbottom boat, maybe ten feet long, with an outboard motor. *The Carbenas?*

Two guys pushed the boat into the water and started the engine. We stood right at the water's edge, waiting for the men to arrive.

A white crane dipped low, gliding in close to the surface of the water, seeming unperturbed by the boat as it bumped into the riverbank.

Ponytail and the kid splashed into the water, grabbed a rope attached to the front of the boat and pulled it further onto the gravel bank.

Fat Man removed the cuffs and said, "Have fun, Hot Shot," and then pushed me forward. As I stepped into the boat, Ponytail said something in Spanish through gritted teeth. I had no idea what he said, but I could tell it was less than complimentary.

So there I was, in a boat with two scary-looking dudes, heading for Mexico. Both had shaved heads and tattoos up and down both forearms. One kept me covered while the other steered the boat as it fought the gentle current and headed toward the group of people on the opposite bank.

The thug with the gun smiled at me and, speaking in a surprisingly good American accent, said, "Welcome to Mexico, Homes."

14

Sunday, July 20, 2019

Evening

Jumping out of the boat and into the river and swimming for it wasn't an option, not even close. Aside from the tattooed guy with the gun, the small army waiting for me on the Mexican side of the border were all armed with automatic weapons. Good swimmer that I was, I still would have been chopped to pieces before I'd gone ten feet. There was nothing I could do except hope that an opportunity would present itself... before some Carbena torture guru came after me with a scalpel.

The boat's motor purred as we neared the Mexican side of the river. The aluminum boat had no seats, so I sat the best I could in the center, facing the thug controlling the motor. He stared at me, grinning and nodding, as if he was mentally measuring me.

"I don't know what you did to deserve what's coming to you, Homes," he said, "but let me give you some advice. If you can get your hands on a gun, you better put a bullet in your own head and end it quick. El Coco sometimes gives folks that option. The smart ones take the bullet and save themselves the pain. You feel me?"

I nodded. "Oh yeah, I feel you," I said. I could hear the exasperation in my voice, and I tried to suppress it. "Your accent is interesting. You're not from around here, are you?"

I know, it sounds... strange, but I really was curious and, I figured if I could keep the guy talking, maybe I could learn something and maybe... just maybe... I could find a way to escape before I had to endure the aforementioned pain.

The tattooed thug laughed. "Nah, man. I ain't from around here. I grew up in Alabama. Most of us spend time stateside, you know? Till we get into trouble and get deported."

"Oh, I see."

"Yeah," Tattoos continued, "then you end up on the streets of Nuevo Laredo, in a country you never seen since you was in diapers, holding funny-colored money. So, when someone named El Coco offers you a job, you take it, Homes. At least I did. I didn't have nothing else."

"And who exactly is El Coco?"

"You'll find out soon enough. I don't want to ruin your first impression. I'll give you a hint, though. *El Coco* is Spanish shorthand for *El Cocodrilo*, for The Crocodile. As in he'll eat you for his lunch, *hombre*."

"Wow," was all I could say to that.

The boat's motor cut off as we hit shallow water, the thug behind me on the front of the boat never saying a word.

Two men with automatic weapons slung across their backs waded into the water to pull the boat onto the river-bank covered with scraggly bushes. Beyond that was what looked to me like a public soccer field.

I was pulled from the boat by one of the men while the other kept his gun trained on me, I guess to make it clear that escape wasn't an option.

I scrambled up the slope onto a hard-packed dirt road to be met by a tall Hispanic man with slicked-back hair and a jet-black goatee that came to a neat point at the tip of his chin. He pointed at me and said something in Spanish.

Tattoos stepped forward. "He wants to know if you've even been to Mexico before."

I glanced at Tattoos and then back to Goatee. "Are you El Coco?"

Tattoos translated for me.

Goatee looked at me with his coal-black eyes for a long minute. Then he laughed. It wasn't a happy, humorous laugh. It was more like that of a dragon about to devour an innocent little goat. Then, too fast for me to dodge, he swung his hand, making contact with my chin. My head twisted to my left with a snap. The world spun around me for a second and a wave of nausea almost over-came me.

I shook my head, spat blood, looked at Tattoos and said, "I'm guessing that was a no."

"Yeah, that was a no."

"Tell him," I said, staring at Goatee, "that I've never been to Mexico before. Tell him that I'd be happy to sample his hospitality and that perhaps we can all get to know one another real well."

Tattoo translated, but I don't think he told him everything, and I found myself wishing my Spanish was better.

Goatee laughed that hungry laugh once again, then barked orders to the men around him. He might not have been El Coco, whoever that was, but he sure as hell was in charge of this particular group.

The two guys on either side of me grabbed my arms and pulled me to one side. Then one of them jabbed a rifle butt into the back of one of my knees, causing my legs to fold, forcing me to my knees, hard.

Goatee barked orders in Spanish and his thugs jumped into action. *What the hell's going on?* I wondered. *Why aren't we leaving?* We were out in the open, not exactly the safest or most defensible position.

One of the trucks was parked a little way further on along the riverbank. Three of his men opened the back and began shouting. Several people, a man and woman, both probably in their forties or early fifties, accompanied by a young woman aged about twenty, jumped down. I figured the trio was a family: mother, father and daughter. They were followed by two young men who appeared to be in their mid-twenties.

All five were dressed in clothes that probably were once quite nice. Now, though, they were ragged and dirty. In fact, the five of them looked as if they hadn't bathed in a month. Was it fear and excitement I could see on their faces? I had no idea. Each of the first three, the family, had a large backpack hanging from their shoulders. The other two men had nothing, other than the clothes on their backs.

The armed thugs led the dirty little group of people to a spot close to the aluminum boat.

Goatee approached the group and said something to the older man, the father, and pointed at his backpack. The old man shook his head and rattled off something I couldn't understand.

Goatee replied in kind, waving his hands, then pointed at the daughter. The more I looked at her, the younger she seemed to be.

Goatee looked again at the man. The man looked down but said nothing.

Then Goatee nodded and looked the daughter up and down as if he was appraising her. She looked terrified and crossed her arms in front of herself. Her mother moved close to her, put her arms around her and hugged her, shaking her head in fear.

The father spoke quickly, his eyes filled with terror. As he spoke, it was obvious to me his words were those of defeat. All three of them dropped their backpacks on the hard-packed dirt.

Goatee looked around at me and gave me a devilish grin, then turned again, said something to the older man and pointed to the boat. The five of them climbed into the boat without saying another word. One of the thugs clambered in after them and started the motor as two more of Goatee's thugs pushed the boat out into the water. We all watched as the boat made its way slowly across the river.

Tattoo stepped closer to me and said, "They pay a lot to get across. Everything they have. They'll probably get caught and be deported back to Mexico by the end of the week. But maybe they will last a little longer, if they're smart, lucky, *and* if they have family that can hide them. Your president has made it very difficult."

I watched the boat as it fought the current, heading toward the riverbank on the US side in the last light of the setting sun.

It all seemed so different from how it was portrayed in the news. People swimming across the river or getting a ride on a boat like this one, or piling into tiny compartments under the floor in a semi-truck. Those were just facts, though, the stuff you see on TV or read about in the daily newspapers.

What I was seeing was real. These people were risking everything to cross the border, and it included making a deal with the devil himself. As I knelt there on the Mexican side of the border, I couldn't help but feel sad, and more than a little concerned, for the five people in the boat.

Suddenly, I heard a horn blaring from somewhere upriver. Everyone in Goatee's group turned to look, and I wondered what was coming?

A large boat, painted different shades of military green, came speeding around the bend. Someone on board must have spotted our little boat and cut the engines, because it slowed quickly and the bow settled down into the water and cruised slowly forward.

Several soldiers stood on the bow, rifles in hand. One of them was manning a large, powerful spotlight, which he swung back and forth, sweeping across Goatee's group, then the small boat.

The Mexican flag was painted on the side of the vessel, its bright red and green barely visible in the quickly dimming light, and a Mexican flag fluttered from a pole at the rear.

My heart started to race. Was this my chance? Would these Mexican soldiers open fire? The military and the cartels were in a state of constant warfare... At least, that's what I'd heard.

My mind began to whirl as I looked quickly around, trying to get my bearings as I began to plan in which direction I'd run if there was a shootout.

The thug operating the motor on the small boat turned and looked at the military craft. He cut off the motor, the boat slowing immediately.

Goatee stepped closer to the river's edge. His men also stepped forward, their weapons ready in hand. Everyone stood tall, feet apart, chests pushed out in a display of power.

I shifted my weight, ready to jump up the moment the shit hit the fan.

Everyone remained still. The military boat's engines were barely turning over as it continued to approach.

The soldier at the front of the craft rotated the spotlight and its beam swung to the right and illuminated the little boat. The thug operating the motor stood tall and stared into the light, an act of defiance. The soon-to-be illegal immigrants shielded their eyes and cowered down in fear.

The beam swung again and slid across the water to illuminate Goatee and his men.

Goatee stood stock-still, his feet apart, his hands balled into fists on his hips as he stared at the soldiers, his eyes glittering in the bright light.

One of the soldiers, a tall man I guessed must be the ranking officer, raised a hand and nodded in Goatee's direction.

Goatee nodded back.

The officer turned his head and said something in Spanish. The boat's powerful engines roared and the craft surged forward and disappeared around the bend, taking with it my last hope of escape.

Those soldiers must have been paid off, I thought. It made sense. How else could the cartels ferry people across the border, out in the open like we were, without anyone ever noticing? I was also willing to bet that people weren't the only things the little boat carried across: terrorists, drugs, weapons, and God only knows what else?

I continued to watch as the thug in the small boat shouted at the people, apparently telling them he'd taken them far enough because, one by one, they clambered over the side and splashed, waist deep, into the water and waded the last few yards to the riverbank as the boat turned around and headed back.

"Come on," Tattoo said. "We're done here. Now you'll meet El Coco."

"I can't wait," I said.

Two guys grabbed my arms, hauled me to my feet and led me to one of the trucks where I was cuffed again and put into the back seat of a four-door pickup, sandwiched between two big guys with guns. Three more of Goatee's soldiers climbed up into the bed of the truck and sat down, their backs to the window.

I was tired and my wrists were sore. It had been a long day. *Hell, is that ever an understatement.*

The driver fired up the engine, and we were immediately assailed by a cacophony of Spanish rap music that blared out of the vehicle's sound system.

The driver, a heavyset man with gray streaks in his hair, punched the gas so hard the truck threw dirt thirty feet or more into the air behind us. Pinned as I was between Thug Number One and Thug Number Two in the back seat, I still fought against being thrown around by this guy's crazy driving. Dust flew up from the other trucks as they raced, side by side, as if in some kind of race away from the river.

We bounced along the uneven ground, racing by a soccer game that had just begun in the dim light of a half-dozen lights on poles. The kids, some of whom were barefoot, stopped playing and waved at the cartel caravan. The driver of my truck stuck his hand out of the window, waved and, with his other hand, honked the horn. It was as if these cartel thugs were local heroes, not kidnappers, extortioners, and all-around violent criminals. One of the thugs in the back of a pickup ahead of us raised his assault rifle in the air and shook it like an '80s freedom fighter.

The sun had set. The sky to the west was ablaze under the orange and red sunset, and I couldn't help but wonder if it was the last sunset I'd ever see.

And what about my family, my father, my friends? Did any of them have a clue I was now in Nuevo Laredo, Mexico? Was I going to die, and my body never recovered?

That was what Shady had planned for me. He'd cut a deal with this El Coco guy to torture and kill me without anyone ever knowing.

The Hero of Chattanooga, now The Butcher of Laredo, gone without a trace. The press would have a field day. They wouldn't believe I was dead and would pester Amanda for months. The more I thought about it, the more I hated Lester "Shady" Tree. He wasn't just exacting his revenge on me personally; he was also delivering his own twisted brand of justice to my family. If I could have, if he wasn't already dead and buried, I'd have killed him myself, only I wouldn't have settled for a quick bullet to the head; I'd have killed him slowly, painfully. I'd have made him suffer.

Which, ironically, was probably what was in store for me.

15

Sunday, July 20, 2019

Evening

T hey didn't bother to put a bag over my head, so I was able to see where we were going. Eventually, we came to a four-lane highway and left the gravel and dirt roads behind us. As we drove on, the trucks dispersed, each turning off the highway in turn. We continued on at a fair rate of speed. I couldn't read the exit signs so I had no idea where we were.

On one side of the road was wilderness: scattered mesquite trees and cacti as large as small cars. Beyond that and below, the river, the Rio Grande, and even farther beyond, the USA, as out of reach for me as the moon.

On the other side were the neighborhoods, vast stretches of low-built concrete and cinderblock dwellings.

Some were brightly painted orange, sky blue and bright green, but most were just gray and depressing, but brightly lit by the streetlamps, the light from which washed over the highway.

The truck finally turned off, past a Pemex gas station, and quite suddenly we were enfolded into one of the neighborhoods.

It was night, but the streets were brightly lit, not just by the streetlamps but also by the stores and shops. There were people everywhere. There were hot dog carts or taco stands on almost every corner where people gathered around either ordering or eating dinner. Every store or food stand had speakers set up on the sidewalk, playing whatever music the owner happened to like, various forms of Latino rap and pop, mariachi and the inevitable American pop and rap. My captors loved it, riding along with the windows down and jigging up and down in time with the beat. That, and the crap blaring inside the truck, was giving me a headache.

I was trying not to think about the fate that awaited me. I had to stay focused. I knew that if a window of opportunity presented itself, I needed to be ready to act fast. Little did I know that a big fat one was waiting for me at the next street corner.

We passed slowly by an exceptionally loud and busy taco stand and, I have to admit, I was distracted by the bright lights and sounds and all the people yelling over one another ordering their tacos when the pickup suddenly slewed to the left, throwing me hard into Thug Number One.

Tires screeched, and I was thrown forward into the

back of the front seat as the pickup slammed into some-thing head-on, bringing us to a sudden and very definite stop.

What the hell was that? I tried to straighten up, but then I heard gunfire, a trio of shots: *pop, pop, pop.* The driver slumped forward over the steering wheel, revealing three holes in the driver-side windshield.

That's when I saw the white Chevy Suburban that had slammed into the right front fender of the pickup, knocking it off course and causing us to run head-on into a concrete barrier.

The Suburban wasn't moving, but that was because the driver and passenger were both out on the street, guns out, systematically and efficiently picking off the rest of the thugs inside the pickup.

I curled up, got as low as I could behind the front seats, hoping one of the bullets wouldn't find me.

Thug Number Two, on my right, opened his door, cursing in English—who knew he spoke English too? As he rolled out onto the street he pulled his gun, came up onto his feet and, staying low, ran around the back of the truck, hoping to flank our attackers, no doubt.

Thug Number One on my left had taken a bullet to the head. The guy in the front passenger seat? I had no idea, but with Number Two now out of the way, I was on my own in the back. This was my chance, and I took it.

I crouched low. Thug Number One on my left was hit at least four or five times more through the open side window as I slid out of the truck and into the street.

Now what? I don't even know where the hell I am.

Thug Number Two was now at the back of the truck,

squeezing off shots over the top of the tailgate, drawing return fire that came in low, peppering his thighs and knees. The thug dropped to the pavement screaming as two more shots slammed into his chest. Whoever was doing the attacking meant business.

I turned to make a run for it, fully aware that I wouldn't get far with my hands still cuffed as they were, but I ran anyway, crossing the street, trying to get away from the shooting. I don't know what the hell I was thinking, but I had to do something. I thought that maybe if I could put enough distance between me and the crazy that was happening back there, I could blend into the crowd, or else find a nice place to hide in the dark and figure things out.

"Oye," someone yelled behind me.

I turned and saw the man in the front passenger seat falling out of the truck, half-stumbling, half staggering toward me. He was hit in the shoulder, but he had a gun in his good hand and had it raised in my direction.

In the back of the pickup, standing up in the bed, the last of the cartel soldiers shuddered under the impact of what had to have been at least three bullets. He twisted around, his weapon flying out into the street as he tumbled out of the truck bed.

People everywhere were screaming and running for cover. Cars were honking and putting on their flashers.

The guy from the passenger seat took two unsteady steps toward me, his arm outstretched, his gun pointed at my chest. I might have been able to make a run for it and dodge the bullet, but I wasn't about to take that chance. Instead, I stood still and raised my handcuffed hands in the air, thinking it was probably my last act on this earth.

I was wrong. Two shots rang out. One hit the man's chest center mass, the other slammed into his gut. He fell to his knees, the weapon falling from his already lifeless hand, clattering onto the pavement.

I turned. The angle of those shots had not come from the direction of the two attackers in the white Suburban. And that's when I saw him, running through the crazed crowd, gun level and steady. A true professional, as always.

"Let's get you out of here, buddy."

"Hello, Bob," I said, smiling, though I felt like shit. "Boy, am I glad to see you."

"Whatever," he said. "You spotted me in Arkansas. You can't be that surprised."

And, yes, he was right. I hadn't expected him to spring me, not like that but, in the back of my mind, I hadn't forgotten that he was out there, somewhere.

"I'm still glad of the help," I said.

"Fine, let's go. The twins will make a diversion, but Carbena kill squads will be all over this area in five minutes or less. We have to move."

I didn't argue. Bob motioned for me to follow and we ran down a narrow side street, away from the chaos. There were more gunshots behind us, but I was sure the only people left alive at this point were the two attackers in the Suburban... the twins, perhaps?

We ran for a full block to a small car parked under a streetlamp. Bob jumped in the driver's seat, and I practically collapsed into the passenger seat.

He fired up the engine, turned immediately right into an even narrower side street, then right again and proceeded to snake his way across the city, one street after another, making what seemed to me to be random turns. The streets he drove were almost always dark, and he drove with his lights off.

"Thanks for getting me out of that mess, Bob," I said, finally, when I figured we were safe. "I thought I was a goner."

"Don't mention it, boss."

I smiled. Just like old times. He always called me that, and I always hated it. Well, I officially hated it. Truth be told, the expression had been growing on me for a long time, and I was beginning to miss it.

"I have a plan," he continued. "Well, the makings of a plan, anyway."

"Good. Does it involve overthrowing the local cartel?" I asked sarcastically.

He flashed me one of his trademark mischievous grins and said, "How'd you guess?"

16

Sunday, July 20, 2019

Late Evening

After a good half hour of driving around in the dark, sticking to side streets, we pulled up in front of a small house, one of a long terrace of concrete homes. Bob called them "Infonavit houses," whatever that meant. Anyway, we parked in the driveway and went inside.

The house was cramped and crude, furnished only with the basics. Bob produced a key for my handcuffs. I nodded my thanks as I rubbed my sore wrists.

"Okay," I said as I went to the fridge and grabbed a bottle of cold water. "You want to tell me what the hell's going on? Where the hell are we and who are the twins you mentioned earlier? I take it they were the guys in the Suburban, right?"

By then I was back in the living room where Bob sat, straddled, on a folding metal chair. He motioned for me to sit down. I took a seat on the couch under the front window.

"First things first, Harry," he said. "You know those people who had you were with the Carbena cartel?"

"That's what I was told. I'd heard the name before. They're pretty big cartel for these parts, aren't they?"

"You can say that again. The Carbenas are one of the biggest cartels in Mexico. Let's just say I have some history with them myself."

"Of course you do," I said dryly. I also knew he was CIA, had been for years. It must have been during his early CIA years, before he was working for me, that he'd been working in Mexico.

"Well, as you've probably put together already, our old friend Shady Tree, whom I hear you killed, by the way, so congratulations, did some work for the Carbenas."

"I didn't kill him. He shot himself, in front of me. But yes, he always did manage to get his fingers in the most dangerous pies."

"You can say that again, boss. I guess they owed him some favors, a lot of favors."

I frowned. "So what about them, the Carbenas? What do you have in mind?"

"Have you heard of a man they call El Coco?"

I nodded. "Yes, The Crocodile, right? But not before today."

"That's him. His real name is Enrique "Ricky" Mendoza, and he's the leader of the Carbenas in this area. He's a bad guy, and I mean really bad, Harry. He's killed a lot of people."

"And I was to be his next victim."

Bob nodded. "Like I said, he must have owed Shady big. He's also a man of his word. Has to be to keep the respect of his soldiers. He won't stop until you're dead."

I rubbed my wrists absentmindedly. "So how did you figure all this out, Bob? I take it you have connections here in Mexico?"

He grinned. "Well, yes and no. I've been down here... before. I don't know Mendoza personally, but when I heard you were being taken to Laredo, I kinda figured something was up, so I crossed the border and started asking around."

"And the twins?"

"Ah yes, them. They'll be busy most of the night, but you'll get to meet them. They're good people. Tito and Tony. They're very good at... what they do."

I decided I didn't have to ask what they did. I saw how quickly and efficiently they neutralized every Carbena on that truck.

"Anyway," Bob continued, "the way I see it, we're going to have to hit El Coco hard so we can get him off your back... for good. Think of it this way, Harry. We'll be doing the world a favor by toppling one of the most terrifying criminal organizations in the world. Well, one small piece of it, anyway."

I thought about it for a minute. What he was proposing was off the charts, and I didn't like the idea one bit, but what the hell. I didn't have a lot of choice, not unless I wanted to spend the rest of my life looking over my shoulder. Bob obviously had a plan. And if this Ricky "*El Coco*" Mendoza was after my head, I pretty much had to go along with it.

I leaned forward on the couch. "Bob, you're not going to believe this... They have someone that looks like me... No, not just looks like me. He's an absolute doppelganger."

He cocked an eyebrow. "Your what?"

"He looks exactly like me. And I mean exactly. If he walked into my house, Amanda would probably walk up and kiss him."

"Wow. That's freaky. How's that even possible?"

I leaned back again and shrugged. I had no answer, other than to say, "It's just one more layer to this crazy mess I'm in."

"Okay," Bob said. "So we'll try to figure it out tomorrow. The twins will be back soon and we can work out a plan. In the meantime, I'm guessing your family and friends will be worried about you. That we can fix right now."

He stood up and handed me a cell phone, an older model flip phone, a burner, with a small screen and actual buttons. I hadn't owned one in more than a decade. Then he fished in his pocket and took out a tiny ziplock envelope and handed it to me. It contained a SIM card.

"Put it in to make your call," he said, "then take it out. They cost like twenty bucks down at the corner store, so we can use a new one every time we make a call. They'll be tracing the call, so don't be too long, okay? I'll give you some space."

I nodded my thanks, and he left the room. I opened the envelope and inserted the card into the phone and smiled to myself as I did so, thinking about what you see in the movies, how at the end of the call they break the phone in half. It makes for good TV, I suppose, but that's not how it works in real life. Breaking the phone in half doesn't do anything more than make the phone unusable. With the battery and SIM card still inside, the phone can still be tracked and located. Remove the battery and SIM and you make it untraceable. Not even Tim, sitting behind a five-thousand-dollar iMac, can trace it.

Truth be told, I kind of missed those old phones with buttons instead of a touch screen... and the invasive practices that come with it.

Amanda answered on the second ring and immediately started crying. I'll spare you the details but, needless to say, she was happy to know I was still alive.

And, as you can probably imagine, it was good to hear her voice, too. I even got to hear Jade crying in the background. The call didn't last long. The authorities would have begun to trace it the minute she answered. She was able to tell me something I'd been hoping wouldn't happen. The killing of those two Laredo cops had already hit the news, and someone was pushing the narrative that I'd orchestrated my own escape.

I didn't know if one of Shady's agents was behind that, but it was a possibility. It was also just as possible that someone in law enforcement, maybe even Lieutenant Booth, had leaked the story to make me look bad.

And, to tell you the truth, I didn't blame anyone for feeling that way. As far as anyone knew, I had killed a respected law enforcement officer in cold blood and engineered the deaths of two more. After all, it was undoubtedly my face on that security footage... Well, not really, but I still had to prove that it wasn't, and I *was* on the run for Pete's sake.

My prime goals, then, were first to get this El Coco guy off my back, then track down my doppelganger. If I couldn't deliver him, the real killer, to the police in Laredo, I'd be a fugitive the rest of my life.

My time with Amanda was short, too short, and made even shorter when she handed the phone to Jacque. I gave her the quick and dirty of the day's events.

"Bob Ryan, huh?" Jacque said. She sounded genuinely surprised, which meant she wasn't the one who'd tipped Bob off.

"TJ says he's going to Nuevo Laredo to work with you, Harry," she continued, "and he says he won't take no for an answer."

I didn't like it, but I wasn't going to argue. I knew it wouldn't do any good. TJ, bless him, was a law unto himself, and besides, an extra pair of hands might come in handy—no pun intended. And, if Bob was right, and we were really going to try to topple a major cartel, we'd need all the help we could get.

I told her I'd call him later, and that was the end of it. Bob came back into the room, tapping his watch, and I could hear Tim shouting in the background that I was probably being traced. So, I said my goodbyes, terminated the call, flipped the phone over, removed the battery and the SIM card, and handed everything to Bob.

"We'd better catch some sleep, Harry. Tomorrow's going to be quite the busy day. You can use one of the bedrooms in the back."

And I did.

17

Monday, July 21, 2019

Morning

After a night of fitful sleep in a hot and humid bedroom with only a small pedestal fan to stir the air, I rose early and hit the shower. The water was cold, refreshing.

I heard Bob leave just as I was getting into the shower. He wasn't gone long, returning with a full change of clothes for me and Starbucks coffee for two.

"They have Starbucks in Mexico?" I asked.

"Yep," he replied. "We need the caffeine. I talked to the twins a few minutes ago. They're bringing breakfast."

I got dressed and joined Bob at the kitchen table, sipping my coffee from the tall cup. After what I'd been through the past several days, it was... heavenly.

"Okay, Harry," he said, and added after several seconds, "let's get down to it."

I smiled and said, "About damn time."

He leaned forward in his chair. There was a fire in his eyes, a look I'd seen many times before. Bob was a man of action, much like TJ in many ways. What we were about to discuss was right up his alley.

"Okay, so the Carbenas have multiple safe houses across the city. El Coco doesn't stay anywhere for too long. He abandons one house then takes another."

"And by take, you mean?"

Bob nodded, confirming my thought.

"They pick a place they like, and either run the owners out or they... disappear them. The authorities are well aware of what they do, but they do nothing about it... They can't. People in high places are paid off, and the local law enforcement has no option but to ignore what's going on."

I couldn't believe what I was hearing. It wasn't as if we were in some war-torn African country. If we had been, I could perhaps have understood what was going on, but we were no more than a ten-minute drive away from the US border for Pete's sake.

Bob produced an iPad, pulled up Google Maps, and then set it down on the table between us.

"You have Wi-Fi here?" I asked, amazed.

"Hey, this is a big city... well, biggish. This is Nuevo Laredo. As I said, it's big, big and ugly. There are lots of places to hide, but I'm betting that this is where El Coco will be..."

He zoomed in on the map to a section of the south

side of the city, farther away from the Texas border. As the labels populated the map, Bob zeroed in on a section called *Centro de Ejecución de Sanciones Nuevo Laredo*. It looked to me like a huge compound, several blocks in each direction, with a group of at least a dozen buildings right at the center and... were those guard towers I could see?

"What the hell is that?" I asked.

Bob grinned. "It's the jail. The Carbenas run it... Like the gangs do many of our prisons. The twins say they have for years. It's basically a cartel stronghold now."

I frowned. "How do the cartels control a jail? Does that mean they let everyone go?"

"No. It's still administrated by the government, and the judicial system still sends criminals there. And the prison guards still make sure no one escapes... at least officially. But outsiders don't go in, not anymore. The Carbenas own the interior, and they can come and go pretty much as they please."

"And you think El Coco is in there?"

"Yeah, that would be my best guess, based on what my sources have told me, anyway. But we need to confirm."

I looked at Bob and smiled. His sources, huh? Spoken like a true CIA spook. I still had trouble seeing him that way, especially after working with him for so many years.

"What's so funny?" Bob asked.

"Nothing. It's just good to have you back."

He scratched the back of his head. "Well, I wouldn't say I'm back. But I couldn't let you hang for something you didn't do."

"Right, right... and thank you for that, at least."

I tried to play it cool. But I knew he probably wasn't back. Not yet, anyway. But still, it was nice to play like old times, even if it was just once more.

I heard a car pull up outside. Bob pulled a gun and slid it across the table at me, before rising to his feet.

I stood up, checked the chamber, and then put my back to the nearest wall.

I heard footsteps approaching the front door.

Bob pulled a second gun from behind the couch and crouched down, his weapon at the ready.

My heart raced. Had they found us?

Then, someone outside whistled, a quick, double whistle, as if he were calling a dog.

Bob relaxed, stood up smiling, slipped the weapon into the rear of his waistband, went to the door, turned the two door locks, opened the door, stepped back, and in walked a short Mexican man with a small mustache and a large smile. I immediately recognized him as one of the two guys who'd saved my ass the night before.

Right behind him was a second man; but for the clothes, he was almost identical to the first. The twins, no doubt.

"Harry, meet Tito and Tony," Bob said. "It doesn't matter which one's which. They're the twins."

I tucked the gun into my waistband, smiling. "Nice to meet you."

"*Mucho gusto*, my friend," the first of the two men said. They were each carrying a plastic bag. Whatever was in them smelled incredible, reminding me how little I'd eaten the last several days.

Right behind them were three familiar faces.

TJ wasn't smiling, but he seemed happy enough to be there, pumping my hand as if he hadn't seen me in years.

Yes, I was surprised to see him. I hadn't told Jacque where we were... because I didn't know; still didn't, so you can imagine how surprised I was to see Jacque walk in right behind TJ, and then Tim, complete with a backpack and a MacBook tucked under his arm.

"Tim? Jacque? What the hell are y'all doing here? How did you find us?"

"Tito and Tony came and picked us up," Tim said.

"But why are you here?" I repeated. "This place isn't safe. You need to go back to Texas right away."

Jacque shook her head. "No, we're staying, Harry. We're going to help you beat dis ting."

"I don't think you understand, Jacque," I pressed. "I'm a fugitive. If we get caught, the police will arrest both of you as accomplices, and probably charge you with obstruction, too. I can't allow that to happen. You need to go back, both of you."

"Take it easy, Harry. We'll be fine," Tim said, setting his laptop down on the table. Then he sat down and opened it. "All we have to do is prove you're innocent. If we can catch the guy who looks like you, we'll all be off the hook. Anyway, we're here now and there's no going back."

I looked at Jacque and said, "Please... Jacque, come on. You can't do this. The Carbenas won't think twice about killing both of you, or worse."

Jacque walked right up to me, her eyes boring into mine, wrapped her arms around my neck, hugged me and said, "You risked everything to save me from Shady; you and TJ and Tim. You all could have died that day. We're a team. All of us, and we stick together and we fight together. So fire me if you want, but I'm not leaving. Besides, I already learned to shoot the last time I had to save your butt from Shady's goons. We'll be fine."

Then she kissed my cheek, turned me loose and joined Tim at the table.

TJ just shrugged and said, "I told them it would be dangerous, Harry. But they didn't give a shit."

"Okay, fine," I said and sighed.

Jacque was right, of course. She had learned to shoot when Shady's men came after me and my family in my home. That was a dark day, and Jacque had unloaded an entire magazine into one thug just as he was about to shoot me. For that I was eternally grateful.

"Thank you," I said to the group. "Thank you all."

"Sit the hell down, boss," Bob said. "We ain't got time for mushy stuff. We have a plan to hammer out."

One of the twins smiled and said, "And besides, we have breakfast tacos."

18

Monday, July 21, 2019

Mid-morning

The tacos were good, better than good. Some were filled with egg and potato, others with different kinds of meat. Little plastic bags of bright red and green salsa were piled in the middle of the table. One of the twins, Tito, I think it was, told us that the red salsa was very spicy, while the green was mild, made with jalapenos and cream.

Thinking back to Maria's love of spicy food, I decided to stay with the green. Jacque bathed her tacos in the red stuff and smiled wider with every bite, even as her eyes watered.

The twins? Bob had known them for more than twenty years, since his early CIA days when he was stationed in Tijuana.

They were... independent contractors which, in real terms, meant they were mercenaries and, based on what I'd seen the previous night, they were damn good at what they did. I was happy to have them aboard.

Bob filled the newcomers in on his basic theory of how, for whatever reason, El Coco was doing Shady's dirty work for him. He also explained that the jail was the Croc's probable stronghold.

When he'd finished his dissertation, Tito nodded and said, "*Si*, the Carbenas control the jail. And they have a small army inside. But I don't think El Coco will be there. He likes to live well."

Tony nodded and said, "Is true."

"Okay," Bob said. "So that's good news, right? If what you say is true, we don't have to break in and out of the jail. I like that. If Mendoza is somewhere else, we take him out and put an end to it. Easy."

Jacque put down her taco and said, "I don't think so, Bob."

We all turned to look at her.

"What do you mean?" Bob asked.

"I mean we have to remember the main objective. We have to clear Harry. Killing this so-called crime boss is... just a part of it."

I nodded. "She's right. We kill El Coco and we get the cartels off my back. But I'll never be able to return to the US unless we can prove I didn't kill that Texas Ranger."

Tim cleared his throat. "I think I can help with that."

My eyebrows shot up. "You can?"

Tim turned his laptop around so we could all see the

screen showing a still from the Denny's security footage. It was of my lookalike.

Bob leaned forward, looked at the screen, then at me, then back at the screen and said, "Harry, my boy. You weren't exaggerating, were you?"

"No, I wasn't. You can imagine how shocked I was when I saw that face, and my father was sitting right beside me. I think he was even more surprised than I was. I've never seen August Starke so rattled. He looked like he'd seen a ghost."

One of the twins shook his head. "It's a fake. Like that... *como se llama?*... ah, Deepfakes. It's all over the news these days, right?"

Tim smiled. "Yeah, I know the term. Putting Nicolas Cage's face in random movie trailers. But, no, this is the original footage. It hasn't been tampered with."

"You sure?" one of the twins asked.

"I'm sure."

The twins looked at each other, frowning.

Bob shook his head and said, "It's uncanny, Harry. Someone out there looks just like you. Sheesh, I hope that's the only resemblance. I sure hate to think there were two of you."

"Bite me," I said.

Tim clicked a button on his computer. The image changed to a man's passport. He was me. Well, almost. In the passport shot, his eyes looked a little different, and his hair was lighter, closer to blond than brown.

We all leaned forward, our eyes glued to the photo. The passport card identified the man as Henry Stern.

"I still don't believe it," Bob said, mostly under his breath. "Even his name is similar."

I nodded. But that was the face, all right. Add a little hair dye on his head, and he'd pass for me just about anywhere.

"I did some... well, let's just say I did a little digging," Tim said. "and used the FBI's facial recognition software." He looked up at me and grinned, then continued, "This guy actually lives in the US, in Laredo, at least I think he does, although he has no address listed there. The address on his passport is a motel in Denton, Texas. But government records show him crossing back and forth between Laredo and Nuevo Laredo at least a couple of times a month. He has no criminal record. Not even a parking ticket."

My mind was racing. "So you mean this Henry Stern, who just happens to look exactly like me, lives in this area, is a law-abiding citizen, and he decides to help frame me by gunning down a Texas Ranger with my gun?"

Tim nodded. "Yeah, basically that's about it. My best guess is he works for the cartels, the Carbenas, and has never gotten caught. So, when Shady came down here to work for them... the Carbenas, he must have run into Henry Stern and come up with an idea to frame you. It's genius, really."

Bob hit the table with his fist. "That's it then. Henry is our guy. We take him alive and turn him in. It won't take the authorities long to piece the rest together, right?"

I nodded. "Yeah... maybe... We need to find this guy and deliver him to the police. And we need proof that he killed that Texas Ranger. It's not much, but it is a plan."

"So," Tim said, "how do we find Henry Stern?"

"Well, that's obvious," Jacque said. "We have to get our hands on El Coco first and squeeze him. He'd gladly turn Henry Stern over to us in return for his life."

I smiled. I liked this grittier side of Jacque, and she was right. If we could get our hands on Ricky *"El Coco"* Mendoza, we'd be able to bargain for both Henry Stern and whatever other proof we needed, but he wasn't going to get away with his life. I couldn't live the rest of my life wondering if he was just around the next corner waiting to kill me.

Tito raised a hand, like a schoolboy in class. "So how do we track down El Coco? He could be anywhere, right?"

Bob grinned. "Well, I was going to mention it earlier, but I got distracted. I have another contact... well, more than one, actually. I'm meeting him for lunch, and I'm hoping he'll know where Mendoza is."

"Okay," I said. "So that's the plan. We talk to Bob's source. We find Ricky Mendoza. We get our hands on Henry Stern and the proof we need to get me off the hook for those murders. Then we all get to go home. Right? Am I missing anything?"

"You are," TJ said. "We need weapons, and not just small stuff, either. We'll need to be loaded for bear."

I looked at TJ and nodded. That old man, seemingly so innocent, was one savage beast with a cold, dark streak somewhere deep inside him, and I had no doubt that he was looking forward to the opportunity to take out some cartel thugs. TJ is like an icy cold wind. You can't stop him. All you can do is harness him so that he works in your favor.

Tony and Tito looked at each other and smiled. "We can get some guns," one of them said. "And equipment, too. Enough for all of us."

"You want to go with me to talk to my source, boss?" Bob looked at me, that oh so familiar playful glimmer in his eye.

I didn't even have to answer. Of course I did, and he knew it.

19

Monday, July 21, 2019

Mid-day

Saturday lunchtime in downtown Nuevo Laredo was an experience. The city was full of life and crazy with people. The sun was high and hot. There wasn't a single cloud in the sky, but the locals didn't seem to care. They walked packed together, jamming the sidewalks, some wearing hats, others carrying umbrellas to provide them a modicum of shade.

Bob and I crossed a plaza lined with trees, past a bench where a young couple was making out. An old man, obviously homeless, dressed in rags and carrying an empty beer can, watched the youngsters as he shuffled slowly by, a lustful grin on his face.

Loud music played from two large, black speakers on the sidewalk outside a nearby store, and a man selling shaved ice stood behind his mobile cart, serving a line of kids and adults.

At the far end of the plaza, across the street, was a diner above which a sign read *Mar La*. Below that were the words *El Hogar del Bisquet*. I had no idea what any of that meant, but it didn't matter since those breakfast tacos were still sitting heavy in my stomach.

We crossed the street and walked inside. The air was cool. Old men sat at tables, drinking coffee and staring at one another like old friends with too much time on their hands do.

Bob led me to the back of the diner where a large man was sitting by himself. He had almost no hair and was wearing a pair of glasses that looked as if they were straight out of the 1970s. Tiny tufts of gray hair stuck out above his ears. His gray mustache was huge, bushy. *What is it about Texas and Mexico and mustaches? Everyone has one.*

The man was... well, he was round. His belly stuck out so far that his incongruously short arms barely reached the table on which was a large plate of what looked like beans, rice, and enchiladas, smothered in white cheese.

"Ah, Roberto," the man exclaimed as we approached. "Take a seat, eh?"

We both sat down, and a young waitress approached and said something in Spanish.

To my surprise, Bob looked up at her, smiled and answered her in impeccable Spanish. The young woman nodded, smiled and walked away.

"I ordered us coffee only. Unless you're hungry?" Bob said with a grin.

"No, coffee is fine," I said. That green salsa may have been mild compared to the red stuff, but it was giving me heartburn.

"Roberto," the man said. "You come to town and there is trouble. Coincidence?"

"No coincidence, I'm afraid," Bob replied, smiling and shaking his head. Then he looked at me and said, "Harry, this is Jose Carmen Moreno. Jose, this is Harry Starke."

Jose Carmen Moreno put a hefty bite of beans and rice into his mouth and chewed, looking me up and down. After he swallowed, he smiled, beans in his teeth, and said, "Call me Joe. All the Americans call me Joe."

"Nice to meet you, Joe," I said.

The waitress came back and put coffee cups in front of us, along with a small metal cup of milk.

"Gracias," I said, using one of the few Spanish words I knew.

"We need information, Joe," Bob said. "We have a common enemy, and we are here to take him down."

Jose's eyes bulged. "You mean..." He paused and leaned forward. Well, he tried to. Unfortunately, his expansive girth restricted his movements, but he tried. Then he continued and whispered the rest of his question. "You are here for El Coco? The CIA?"

Bob shook his head. "Not the CIA. Just me and my friends."

Jose frowned, bobbing his head as if weighing the concept in his head. "Okay, I will help you. Plenty of people would be happy to see that one gone. He is vicious."

"We need to know where he is," I said.

Joe looked at Bob, then at me, then took another big bite of food. Some of the food missed and ended up on his chin, slowly running down the curve toward his collar.

"I heard something today," Joe said finally. "I don't know if it is true, but it makes sense."

"What's that?" Bob asked.

"Well, you made trouble for him yesterday, Roberto. He doesn't know you. He doesn't know who you are working for. The word on the street is that he is doing a favor for an American crime boss. A man they say is already dead. Can you imagine? How can that be?"

"Yeah," Bob said dryly. "We can imagine."

Joe looked at me. "You know about the favor?" Then his eyes got wider as recognition blossomed on his face. I began to get a sinking feeling as the man's features twisted first into shock and then anger.

"Hey, I've seen you before," he snarled.

Bob and I looked at each other, confused.

Joe waved his hand, and, suddenly, five men from the tables surrounding ours stood up and advanced on us.

How did we not notice them before? They wore loose, button-up shirts, untucked. Perfect for hiding a firearm. In fact, as one shifted weight, I could see the bulge of a gun on his hip.

"You are..." Joe snapped his fat fingers, trying to recall the name. "You are Stern. Son of a bitch, Roberto. I am disappointed. You are working with El Coco now? Damn. I didn't want to have to kill you."

I shook my head. "Joe, this is a mistake. I'm not Henry Stern. My name is Harry Starke. I'm from Tennessee. I've never set foot in Mexico before yesterday."

Joe squinted at me. "Prove it."

Bob raised a hand. "Joe. I'm not working for Mendoza. You know me better than that. Remember Veracruz? Toluca? What about that time I saved your ass in Tijuana? I don't work with trash like El Coco."

Joe studied Bob's features. Hell, I didn't know he'd spent so much time in Mexico. The man had some stories to tell, and one day... maybe.

Finally, Joe looked back at me. "Harry Starke, huh? What do you know of El Coco?"

I shrugged. "Not much, but I can tell you this. He's doing the favor for a man named Lester Tree. And yes, he's dead. I watched him kill himself a month ago. He arranged for me to be framed for a murder I didn't commit and for the Carbenas to kidnap me once they brought me to Laredo. I'd be dead right now if it wasn't for Bob."

Joe concentrated, taking in everything I said. Finally, he turned down the corners of his mouth, nodded slowly and said, "Okay, so you're not Stern? But you look like him."

"That's the problem, Joe," Bob said. "They're using this Stern guy to incriminate Harry. We have to take Mendoza out, find Stern and turn him over to the police in Laredo so Harry can go home to his family."

Joe waved the men away. They returned to their lunch, as if nothing had happened. I didn't think the old men close to the door even noticed what had happened.

"I believe you, Roberto," Joe said. "Besides, sending just two men after me isn't Ricky Mendoza's style. He would send an army of guys to throw grenades in through the windows. That is how he operates. It's distasteful, no? Even the CIA works cleaner than him, and the *Americanos* are messy sons of bitches."

"No offense taken," Bob said with a grin.

I breathed easy. Something told me that, whoever this Jose Carmen Moreno guy was, we'd just dodged one hell of a big bullet.

"So can you help us?" Bob asked.

Joe seemed to ignore the question and went back to his lunch.

I sipped my coffee.

"I can tell you what I know," Joe said, finally, between bites. "Mendoza thinks someone big is after him. He is scared. If he knew you at all, Roberto, he'd be even more afraid. He is holed up in a safe house near the jail. He is safe there, he thinks."

Bob and I looked at each other.

We'd hoped El Coco wouldn't be in the jail because the place was obviously a stronghold. So this was good news.

Joe pulled a small notebook and pen from the breast pocket of his button-down shirt, a garment that was easily two sizes too small for the man. He scribbled a note, tore out the page, and handed it to Bob.

"The address," Joe said. "I hope the info is good. It

would do this town a lot of good if Mendoza's head were to end up on a stick, Roberto. And if anyone can do that, you can."

"Thanks, Joe. I'll take that as a compliment."

Joe shrugged and went back to eating. Bob and I looked at each other, quickly finished our coffee and stood up. This conversation was done, apparently.

Bob reached into his pocket and pulled out a wad of bills, Mexican money, bright orange in color.

Joe shook his head, waving Bob away. "I will pay for your coffees. It is the least I can do. Just do me this favor, Roberto. When you have that monster in your grasp, before you kill him, break his nose and tell him it was from me. He'll know why."

Bob nodded. "Thanks, Joe."

We turned and headed out of the diner and into the sunshine.

We stood for a moment at the curbside as a bus filled with locals drove by. Most of them were talking and laughing with each other in their colorful clothing. The people of Nuevo Laredo had no idea of the war that was about to hit the town.

20

Monday, July 21, 2019

Afternoon

We drove back to the house using only the back roads, so it took a while. On the way, I couldn't help but poke fun at Bob a little.

"So, Roberto, huh?" I said. "Is that your Mexican code name? Like Zorro, but less cool?"

Bob grinned. "Hey, Jose is a friend. Even if he is a slob. He wants what's best for Mexico, and he's worked with the CIA several times, and I've saved his ass more than once. He owed me. I was just happy that he was here in town. More often than not, he's in Mexico City or Puebla."

"You know, we've never discussed it. You dropped it on me and disappeared, but I was surprised when you told me about your CIA background, Bob, and the more I learn, the more surprised I become."

"Well, just be glad we have the intel," Bob said, as he tapped his jacket over the inside pocket that held the slip of paper Jose had given him. "With this we can build a plan."

And that's exactly what we did. We gathered around the table as Tim entered the address in Google Maps on his laptop and showed us an image of the house.

It was a big, yellow two-story building located just across the street from the side entrance to the jail.

Tito looked at the image and shook his head, clicking his tongue. "That's bad news, guys."

"Why?" I asked.

"I know that place. It is a fortress, just like the jail. Google Maps does not show it, but that place is full of soldiers."

Tony nodded. "Yeah, the Carbenas are well-armed. They have fifty caliber mounted machine guns. Grenades. Rocket launchers. Everything, man. They see us there and they will blow us all away."

"Then we don't allow them to see us," I said.

"I agree," Bob said. "So how do we pull that off?"

"Well," Jacque spoke up. "I have a question. What does this *Coco* do all day?"

Tony cocked his head to one side and said, "What do you mean?"

"I mean is he going to just stay inside that house all day long? Every day? Forever?"

"No," Bob answered. "He has a pretty active social

life, I think. He plays golf, occasionally, goes to parties and... Hell, I don't know. Stuff. Right?"

He looked at Tony.

"He meets with his men, too," the twin said. "If he's scared, like your source said, then he probably will go out only at night."

"Okay," Jacque said. "So, we watch the house. We wait for him to leave and we grab him when he's out in the street, right? Easy, right?"

I frowned. "Well, not easy. But yeah, Jacque, that's a good point. We watch the house." I turned to Tony and continued. "Can you guys get surveillance equipment?"

Tony nodded. "Sure can, boss."

I narrowed my eyes at him, throwing a thumb in Bob's direction and said, "Call me Harry, Tony."

"Okay, *por Dios*. Sorry." Tony was smiling.

Bob shot me a look and said, "Okay, enough with that. We have a plan. I'd imagine El Coco doesn't go anywhere without an entourage. But it would be easier to fight them in the open than try to take the house."

"So, can we start tonight?" TJ asked. "We start watching the place, and when he moves, we move in and snatch him."

We all nodded.

"Let's do it," I said.

Jacque and Tim continued to work on his laptop. TJ conferred with Tony and Tito. He was interested in learning about the weapons they secured. Like Tim, TJ loves his toys but, unlike Tim, the aging vet's idea of "toys" included fully automatic assault rifles, military-grade explosives, and knives that could pass for machetes.

It was at times like those that TJ kind of worried me. He seemed just a little too bloodthirsty, and yet, he'd saved my bacon more than once. He may have enjoyed what he did a little too much, but he always seemed to know when to stop... well, so far, anyway. I dreaded the day TJ would cross the line and I'd have to stop him. Much like an overly aggressive dog, there's only so much you can allow before you have to do something about it.

Bob beckoned me to one side and whispered, "You know," he said, "Jose was about to kill us because of how much you look like that Stern guy."

"Yeah, I know. It was kind of scary."

"Too bad the Carbenas know you have a doppel-ganger. Otherwise, we could just walk you into that compound pretending to be Stern."

I nodded. "You think?"

"How is it this guy looks so much like you, anyway?" Bob asked.

I shrugged. "It isn't that unusual, is it? Hitler had several doubles. So did Patton, I believe. And... I dunno... It just happens, I guess."

"Yeah, I suppose. But this guy *really* looks just like you. I can't get my head around that. Can you?"

Again, I shrugged. "I don't know, Bob. So many crazy things happen in our lives. I guess this is just one more."

"Okay, but if I were you, I'd be asking your pop if you have a secret twin."

I smiled. "Secret twin. Right. Cut it out, Bob. This is serious stuff. We have a crime lord to kidnap."

He shook his head and said, "Okay, you're the boss, Boss." Then he turned and walked out of the room, leaving me wondering just who the hell was Henry Stern.

When this is over... I'm going to find out.

21

Monday, July 21, 2019

Evening

The hot afternoon rolled on and turned into an almost-as-hot evening. *Is there ever a breeze in this god-awful place? I mean, Tennessee summers can get to me, but Mexico is downright oppressive.*

By seven o'clock that evening, everything was in place. We all had burner phones so that we could communicate with one another—not quite up to the standard of Tim's comms units, but they would do the job—and, as long as we didn't call anyone outside of our little group... well, you get the idea. And they were cheap. As far as I could tell, the whole shebang cost less than a hundred bucks.

By the time Bob and I drove to the lookout point, the

sun was already low in the western sky. It was going to be a beautiful, if very warm, evening. We'd all agreed that we, Bob and I, would take the first shift and let everyone else get some well-earned rest.

When I left, Tim looked like he was going to pass out from the heat. Jacque, on the other hand, looked right at home. The Caribbean heat was in her blood, I guess, so she was used to it.

The lookout spot was a semi-derelict two-story house located just a couple of blocks from the substantial, yellow fortress El Coco currently called home.

"Lots of houses around this city look like this," Bob explained. "The people that lived in them were either killed or carted off by the cartels... or by the Mexican military."

We parked around the corner, grabbed our gear, which we'd bundled into two military backpacks, and slipped through a gap in the concrete wall that surrounded the house.

The house must have been abandoned for years. The once landscaped yard was overgrown with tall weeds and grass except for one small area where the weeds had been trimmed, and a pile of old clothes, well flattened, appeared to be someone's makeshift bed.

In the gathering darkness, as we crossed the little garden at the rear of the house, I noticed something. The walls were peppered with bullet scars. There were dozens of them. Some small, from rifles or handguns, no doubt, and some big enough to put my fist through, obviously the handiwork of a high-caliber mounted machine gun. Whatever had gone down here, sometime long ago, it couldn't have ended well for the occupants.

The rear door had been bricked up. Concrete blocks, cemented in place, filled the opening where the doorway had been. The windows, too, were similarly closed off.

Bob pointed at the blocks and said, "That's to keep out squatters. It also means the house has been confiscated by the government. C'mon. We get in from round there, I hope."

We worked our way around the building to a flight of ornamental iron stairs that led to a small balcony on the upper floor. From there, an iron ladder anchored to the wall took us up to the flat, concrete roof.

On the roof was a large, black plastic water tank and two T-shaped poles with wire clotheslines stretched between them. Other than that, the roof was a wide-open space with a waist-high perimeter wall. It was just about perfect!

We picked a spot at a corner of the roof that provided a view of the gated entrance to El Coco's fortress and settled down to watch... and wait.

We had binoculars with night-vision and a radio scanner.

We took turns watching the house. While one of us watched, the other wore the headset and listened to the scanner. Me? I wasn't sure I should be listening to the radio.

"It all sounds like gobbledygook to me," I said.

Bob shrugged. "Most of it isn't Spanish anyway. I don't understand it, either. They speak mostly in code, using nonsense words. But when and if Mendoza leaves, we should hear a massive boost in the chatter."

Time passed slowly. I spent most of my turns with the binoculars studying the fortress. It was huge, and I wondered who the unlucky owner was. Parts of the building were three stories, and there were at least two outbuildings that I could see, all surrounded by a wall that had to be at least eight feet high. Almost all the great houses—the few I'd seen—were walled, but this one was taller than most, and there were guard towers built just inside the walls populated by heavily armed guards. In fact, the place was teeming with them. *Me thinks El Coco has a paranoia problem.*

There were also several trucks parked in the court-yard, each with a mounted gun and a bored-looking, sleepy thug sitting in the truck bed.

I imagined us trying to storm that fortress. From what little I could see, I figured we'd need at least a dozen men and some seriously heavy weaponry. *And there's no telling how many more there are inside the building,* I mused.

"So what have you been up to, Bob?" I asked during a lull in the chatter—it was my turn with the headphones. "It's been months since our last chat."

"Oh, you know how it is," Bob said. "I've been trying to figure things out."

"What's there to figure out?"

"Well... I kind of opened some channels from my CIA days, channels that probably should have stayed closed. But there was this case... I've been thinking about it a lot lately, something that happened years ago, before I

met you and, well, I don't know..." He swept the binoculars back and forth.

"What case?" I asked.

"I... not today, Harry. Let's just say someone took
something from me..." He shook his head, then said,
"Maybe I'll tell you one of these days. It's not something I
want to talk about right now. Know what I mean?"

I nodded. "I know what you mean. We all have 'em.
Cases that stay stuck in the back of your mind and
surface every once in a while, usually when you least
expect it. Well, I hope you can get it figured out."

"Yeah, me too... Actually, it's how I learned about
your arrest, from one of my old contacts."

"Really? I was sure one of my team had called you."

Bob grinned. "Nah. Not possible. When I left you, I
shut down all of my channels. I couldn't afford to get into
trouble and have it lead back to you or Jacque or... Tim.
No, none of your people would have been able to reach
me, not even Tim."

"Really? Sounds to me like you're looking for
trouble."

His grin grew wider as he shook his head. "Now you
know me, Harry. When did I ever run from a fight?"

He was right. Bob Ryan was one tough son of a gun,
and he often leapt feet first into the fray, especially when
one of his friends was in trouble. It's how we first met. He
came out of nowhere and saved me from some nasty
thugs. I never did learn how he did that.

"Well, when you get it figured out, Bob, you're always
welcome back on the team. We miss you, and we could
use you."

"I appreciate that, boss... And you never know, right?"

I nodded.

It was at that moment that we heard loud music echoing up from the street below. I jumped to my feet and grabbed my binoculars just in time to see a limo arrive at the entrance to the fortress, its sunroof open, and we could see bright flashing lights keeping time with the music.

"Well, would you look at that," Bob muttered as we watched the limo pull right up to the gate. The limo's back door opened and a girl jumped out, prancing around, waving her arms in the air. She was followed by another girl, and another until... I counted nine of them, all dancing, singing and yelling.

"Looks like someone's having a party," I said as two thugs with guns slung on their backs opened the front gate and the girls marched in, screaming and laughing, each wearing a tight mini dress that left little to the imagination.

Some of the women were thin as rails, while others were heavy and curvy. Some had short hair, spiked up in a pixie cut, and others had long, curly locks that flowed over their shoulders, almost to their waists.

The thugs watched appreciatively as the girls filed by, dancing into the house.

Then, as the last girl entered the house and the door closed behind her, the two thugs closed the gate, the limo drove away, and the music started up again inside the house, muted but unmistakable. The fortress had become Party Central.

I looked at Bob and said, "I don't think El Coco's going anywhere tonight, do you?"

"With all those fine ladies? Nah. He's going to be busy."

We got comfortable, watching and listening to the radio scanner anyway, taking nothing for granted.

After several minutes, I turned my head and looked over at my one-time partner and said, "You know you can call me if you ever need help? I'll be there for you, Bob."

"Thanks, boss," he said, without taking his eyes away from his binoculars. "That means a lot. I just might take you up on it."

22

Tuesday, July 22, 2019

Early morning

I t was a long night, and the rhythm of Hispanic pop music emanating from the fortress never slowed.

Bob and I passed the time watching and trying to work out the patterns and timing of the guard shifts and patrols. But there seemed to be no rhyme or reason behind any of the comings and goings of the guards, or the patrols. They came, they went, they came again and... it was about as unorganized as anything I'd ever seen. It seemed to me that firepower was the main focus of El Coco's security. His philosophy seemed to be more is better, and even more is better still.

And then there were the cars, small, mostly beat-up cars without license plates that arrived at the house every thirty minutes or so. The gate would open a crack and a punk kid with his baseball cap turned sideways would run into the house carrying a small bag, then run out again a few minutes later, jump back in the car, and speed away.

The place was a hive of activity. The partying went on into the night. We could hear the music loud and clear, and we were two full blocks away. The neighbors were probably used to it, I guess. Either that or they all moved away, which seem to be most likely, because even in the dark, I figured there were at least seven more houses on the street that had been abandoned and bricked up.

It was almost two-thirty in the morning when Bob received a text from Tony, telling him that they were heading out to relieve us, which was good because by then I was beginning to drag.

Usually, I can stay awake for a couple of days, if I have to. But after what I'd been through the past several days, I was bone tired. And I knew that any sudden confrontation with El Coco and his men would be... dangerous, no, disastrous.

It was just after three when TJ and Tony finally arrived, and Bob and I were able to slip silently away, down the ladder, then the stairs and across the garden to the break in the wall.

In the moonlight, I noticed an old man with a Santa Claus beard leaning against the wall in the corner of the garden, close to the ratty clothes and plastic bags, his hand wrapped around a bottle of Don Pedro. At that moment I would have given just about anything for even a taste of Laphroaig.

When this is all over, I promised myself.

Everyone was asleep when we arrived back at the safe house. I waited outside as Bob went in to retrieve a fresh SIM card from his stash. It was the middle of the night. Bad timing, I know, but I didn't want to sleep without hearing Amanda's voice. I dialed her number and was surprised when she answered on the first ring.

"Harry? Is that you?"

"It's me, beautiful. How are you, sweetheart?"

"Oh, Harry, I'm so worried about you. Did Jacque and the boys make it okay?"

"They did. I can't talk long."

I told her we were fine, and I reassured her that we had a plan. I couldn't tell her the details. I knew her phone was probably being recorded by the authorities and that they were running a trace on my phone as we spoke. I doubted the information would do them any good though. I was still in Mexico. Still, Texas Rangers had been known to hunt across the border, and I was taking no chances.

"Your father is here. He wants to talk to you."

"Oh, okay," I said, surprised. I'd figured August would be in a ritzy hotel in Laredo, not slumming it in some vacation rental with Amanda and Kate.

"Are you safe, Harry?"

I reassured him I was... Well, as safe as you can be with one of the deadliest criminal organizations in the world breathing down your neck.

"You need to turn yourself in," he said. It was the company line, of course. He had to say that for the benefit of anyone who might be listening to the call, now or later, perhaps even in a court of law.

"I know, I know. And I will. I just have to get this cartel off my back first, and I have to deliver my lookalike to the authorities. Otherwise, Wyatt Earp and his partner won't give me the time of day to explain myself. Not after everything that's happened."

August was silent for a moment, then said, "I hope you know what you're doing, son. You're dealing with some very dangerous people."

For a moment, I wasn't sure if he was talking about El Coco and his associates or the Texas Rangers and Laredo police. Either way, he was right.

"Don't worry. I'll be careful. And I have backup. Now, you know my lookalike's name is Henry Stern, right?"

Another moment of silence. August was weighing how much he could say. But Bob was also back outside and giving me the evil eye. Time was running out.

"Yes," August said. "I received an email... from an anonymous source."

"Have the police look him up. He's practically my clone. They need to put out a warrant for his arrest."

There was another reason I needed the police looking for Henry. If they didn't find him on the US side of the river, then he was probably holed up with El Coco. Whatever. One way or the other, I needed him to be caught.

"I'll take care of it. You need to go."

"Thanks, Dad."

I grinned at Bob. He was practically jumping up and down.

"Give Jade a kiss for me."

And I ended the call. Bob snatched the phone away from me and pulled out the battery.

"Jesus, Harry. You sure as hell like to live life on the edge, don't you?"

"Oh, come on, Bob," I protested. "They trace the call and see I'm in Mexico. So what? It's not like a SWAT team can just drive across the bridge and break down our door."

"You don't know shit, Harry. It wouldn't be SWAT. It would be DEA or the Marines."

I arched an eyebrow. "The Marines? What are you smokin'?"

"Take it from someone that knows," Bob said, pointing a thumb at his own chest. "The US has people on this side, and they keep 'em here all the time. It ain't publicized, and it probably ain't with Mexican permission, but you can bet your ass, if they figure out where you are, they'll send someone to pick you up... or take you out."

I thought about Bob's impeccable Spanish and his history working with the CIA in Mexico. I thought about the twins, too, freelance mercenaries that worked with Bob. *Doing what, exactly, I wonder?*

"Okay, I get it." I threw my hands up in defense. "I'll keep the phone calls shorter next time."

Bob nodded. "I hope we can end this soon, boss. If we don't, we'll have to relocate to another house in a different part of town. Those Carbenas are smart. They'll figure out where we are sooner or later. Our people are even smarter; you'd better believe it."

"I'm sure you're right, Bob. But all we can do now is wait."

Bob grinned. "That, and sleep. C'mon."

He nodded for me to follow him around the side of the house.

"Where are we going?" I asked.

"Well, since all your friends arrived there aren't enough beds. Plus, it's too hot in there, unless you're right in front of a fan. It's cooler out here in the breeze."

The backyard was small and dark, but two small trees cast dark shadows on the grass.

Bob grabbed a bundle from a patio table by the back door. "You want the sleeping bag or the hammock?"

That's when I noticed the hammock hanging between the trees.

I smiled. "If I have a choice, I'll take the hammock."

Bob nodded. "Probably best. I'm too big and heavy for that thing, anyway. I prefer to sleep on good old terra firma." Then he glanced at me and pointed to my torso. "Although, I've noticed you're getting a bit pudgy around the middle, too, boss, a bit of a dad bod."

"Hey, I'm a father now, remember? I got responsibilities." I rubbed my belly protectively.

"Whatever you say, boss. Whatever you say."

I grunted at him and then climbed into the hammock.

The breeze was nice. Not as good as it had been up on the roof, but it was good enough and, before I knew it, I was fast asleep, a deep, dreamless sleep.

23

Tuesday, July 22, 2019

9am

I t was almost eight when I woke that same morning, less than four hours after I'd hit the sack, but I felt better than I had in days.

Bob woke only minutes after I did, and we both went into the house and took turns in the shower. Jacque was already up and preparing coffee. Bless her.

Tim was still asleep. Jacque explained that he'd been up until late, almost as late as we were, in a world all his own, tapping away on his laptop doing, and achieving, who knew what.

Tito, the twin who'd stayed home, arrived around nine with a brown paper bag, wet with grease. Inside were hot corn tortillas, a wad of napkins, a dozen or so packets of salsa and what looked like chopped cilantro and onion, and a large hunk of shredded meat bundled in aluminum foil.

"It is barbacoa," Tito said. "Only sold on Sundays. It is... heavenly."

I eyed the meat as Tito unwrapped it. It looked like pulled pork but was darker in color. "What animal is this from?"

"Cow." Tito smiled. "What part of the cow? You do not want to know."

"Ah. I see. Well... okay."

As we sat down to eat, I noticed a duffel bag by the front door, something Tito had brought in with the barbacoa. More weapons?

We hadn't been seated long when Tim came shuffling in from a back bedroom. He was dragging, but he perked up when he saw the meat and the rest of the food.

"Well, good morning, everyone," he said, sitting down and grabbing a tortilla.

"You like barbacoa, *amigo*?" Tito asked.

Tim took a big bite of the juicy tortilla and swallowed it almost without chewing. "I'm so hungry, I'd eat a dead dog between two loaves of bread," he said before taking another bite. "Just don't tell me what's in it until I'm done... I'd still rather have Doritos though."

I laughed at that. Tim wasn't a kid anymore. He was a young man in his mid-twenties, old enough to be a father, but he still ate like the teenager I'd hired all those years ago.

Jacque looked at me across the table and said, "So, Harry, how did it go last night? Did you learn anything new?"

"They like to party," I said, "and girls. They were still going strong when we left at three this morning. I don't know how they do it."

"It's all a show," Tito said. "They have to pretend they are having a good time."

Tim frowned. "Why? Who cares?"

"You have to understand, *amigo*. All the kids in Mexico want to be *narcos* when they grow up. They want to be drug lords, hit men, *soldados, halcones*. It is all propaganda."

"*Halcones?*" Jacque asked.

"They're kind of lookouts, right? They keep an eye on what's going on. Like, practically every city in Mexico has them."

Tito nodded. "Yes. *Halcon* means falcon in Spanish. Just like falcons have sharp eyesight. These guys keep an eye out for the cartels. They always know what is going on. They ride motorcycles and use walkie-talkies. They are always watching, listening, and they report everything they see and hear."

I nodded. "In code, right?" I said, thinking about the strange transmissions we heard on the scanner.

"*Si*. That is why the soldiers and police can never surprise them," Tito continued. "The *halcones* track their every movement, twenty-four-seven."

I remembered the look of mutual respect between Goatee and the officer on the riverboat, and I figured the *halcones* weren't the only reason the military hadn't broken up the cartels. *Just how many officials around the country are being paid off, I wonder? The number must be enormous.*

"Anyway, the cartels are winning the popularity contest," Tito continued. "More young kids want to be Carbenas than soldiers. They want to be El Coco instead of *el presidente*."

"I get it," Jacque said. "When the bad guys are more popular than the good guys, the bad guys will be in control."

"The day's coming when the president of Mexico will be the winner of a cartel turf war instead of an election," Bob said.

I leaned back in my seat, my hunger satisfied. The barbacoa was good. Greasy but good.

"That doesn't bode well for the common people, does it?" I asked.

Tito was about to say something, but his phone beeped, a sound I hadn't heard since the late nineties. He flipped the phone open with a snap.

"*Bueno*?"

We all looked at one another, waiting, as Tito listened.

"*Si. Gracias.*"

And then he was up and out of his chair, even before he snapped the phone closed.

"El Coco is on the move," he said.

Tito grabbed the duffel bag, opened the door and ran outside, Bob no more than a step behind him. I jumped up and was about to follow them when Jacque also leaped up from her seat, as did Tim, wiping his mouth with a paper napkin.

"Oh, no," I said. "You two are staying here."

"No way, Harry," Jacque said. She pulled a gun, a

shiny 1911 .45, from her waistband. It looked like a cannon in her small hands. "TJ took me to the range before we left. I'm good to go."

"I'm sure he did," I said dryly. Actually, I knew Jacque didn't need lessons. After I'd first taught her how to shoot, more than a year ago, she'd been to the range two or three times a week. She was almost as good of a shot as I was.

"No!" I snapped. "It's too dangerous, for you and for Tim."

"But we came to help, Harry," Tim protested.

"I know, and you're helping a lot, but you're not going out there to get yourselves killed."

I glared at them hard enough to let them know I meant it.

Jacque glared back at me, then nodded, the look of disappointment plain on her face.

"Just watch out for each other, okay?" I said.

Then I turned and ran out through the open door.

Tito and Bob were already in the car with the engine running. I jumped in the back seat, next to the duffel bag, and opened it as Tito drove out onto the street, tires squealing.

Just as I expected. Inside were three Israeli Tavor TAR 21 fully automatic assault rifles, a dozen fully loaded magazines, and enough ammunition to supply a small army. *No wonder it took two of them to carry it out.* The bag also contained two vests. I looked at Bob and Tito. Tito was already wearing his vest. I passed one over to Bob and put the other one on myself.

"What's happening, Tito?" I asked.

"El Coco left the compound in a white Lincoln Navigator five minutes ago. There are two trucks with him, one in front and one behind."

Tito was talking fast and driving fast. The tires squealed as he slung the vehicle around a corner.

Bob flipped open his phone and hit a number on the speed dial. It must have been Tony who answered because he began speaking rapidly in Spanish, and then Bob spoke in Spanish to Tito. I figured Tony must have been giving him directions.

Me, I checked the weapons, made sure they were loaded and ready to fire with just a click of the safety, then I passed two of them to Bob. He lay both of them across his lap, then grabbed the strap above his door as Tito threw the vehicle into another wild turn.

I learned later that Tony and TJ were following El Coco, forwarding street names to Bob who, in turn, gave them to Tito. No more than ten minutes later, we were in position and set up for a classic Pincer attack.

"We'll come in hot," Tito said in English, for my benefit. "We need to block the SUV or shoot out the tires. Then we need to take out the guards."

I nodded. My heart was racing.

"Use the car as cover," Bob said. "The trucks don't have mounted guns, so nothing will go through the car."

Tito rounded a corner and slowed almost to a stop.

"Wait... wait... wait," Bob whispered.

I looked out the side window and saw a boy of about twelve walking down the street in a faded Blink 182 T-shirt, tattered shorts, and flip-flops. He carried a clear plastic bag of food in one hand and a two-liter bottle of

Coca-Cola in the other. A small brown dog, little more than a puppy, was at his heels on a piece of string, its tongue lolling out. Unfortunately, they were approaching the corner where we'd planned to launch our attack.

"Wait," Bob whispered again.

The puppy jumped up, trying to lick the boy's face as he walked. The boy laughed. They continued on toward the corner.

"Wait," Bob repeated.

Farther down the street, an old woman was sweeping the sidewalk in front of her house. Behind us, a man carried out a bucket of soapy water and a sponge to his car, a Volkswagen Beetle that looked old enough to belong in a museum, and began to wash it. *Geez, this is falling apart.*

"Wait," Bob said again.

The wait was killing me.

"Go, go, go!" Bob yelled.

Tito punched the gas.

I grabbed my TAR 21 and flipped off the safety.

24

Tuesday, July 22, 2019

11am

The car lurched forward, its tires squealing, past the boy and the dog and the old woman with the broom in a blur.

We reached the corner. Tito swerved across the street and slammed on the brakes, blocking the intersection. The Carbena pickup truck came to a screeching stop, honking its horn.

Even before we'd stopped, Bob had rolled down his window. Tito jumped out and raised his rifle over the roof of the car. Bob, still in the car, positioned his weapon and all hell let loose.

Now, unless you spend any time at all around guns which, unfortunately, I do, you can't possibly appreciate just how loud the report of a rifle is, the more so in an enclosed space.

The movies play lots of loud bangs and booms in their meticulously choreographed firefights, but the volume doesn't even come close to that of an actual firearm. Ready as I was, and as experienced as I was, even I was taken by surprise by the cacophony created by Bob's weapon inside the vehicle.

The windows rattled as the two CIA-trained killers picked off the Carbena soldiers before they could even raise their weapons. Bob peppered the windshield, killing the driver and his two companions, which was good because the truck wasn't going anywhere without its driver. But it was also bad because the driver's now dead foot fell off the brake pedal, and the idling pickup rolled towards our car until it finally ran gently into my door.

Bob scrambled across the driver's seat and out onto the street.

I scrambled across the back seat, my ears ringing, and opened the other door and rolled out onto the road, falling heavily on my back, rifle in hand, and just in time, too; a stream of bullets hammered into the car, showering me with shattered glass as I hunkered down.

I looked at Bob crouched down beside me, Tito beside him. He nodded. We waited for a pause in the shooting, then the three of us jumped up together and opened fire, killing the two soldiers standing in the truck bed.

I heard more shooting coming from beyond the truck. Tony and TJ were engaging the soldiers in the pickup behind El Coco's SUV.

Tito scrambled up onto the hood of the cartel's pickup, a red stain slowly spreading on his shoulder. He'd been hit, but he didn't seem to notice. He crested the hood, rested his rifle on the top of the pickup's cab, and opened fire.

I ran around the rear of the car. Bob went in the opposite direction, around the front, and we moved forward, laying down short bursts of covering fire as we went.

I dropped the first mag, inserted another, and continued on. The Luxury SUV was slewed across the road just behind the pickup. The second pickup was just beyond the SUV.

I put two bullets in the right front tire of the SUV, flattening it. A thug leaned out of the Navigator passenger side window, pistol in hand. I put a burst of three bullets in his upper torso. He hung limp out of the window.

The back door of the SUV opened and my heart skipped a beat, as out tumbled a scared and panicking Henry Stern, a gun in one hand, both hands in the air. He was followed by a second man.

The second man was tall and thin with dark skin and rugged features, black hair buzzed short. He looked to be in his fifties. He was wearing... would you believe a silver sharkskin suit, black shirt, open almost to his waist and a heavy gold chain around his neck. He couldn't have looked more like an '80s action movie bad guy if he'd tried... and maybe he was, trying. All that was missing was the ponytail.

This, then, was El Coco.

He had a smartphone to his ear and a mini-Uzi in his right hand, and he was swinging it in my direction.

I jumped back behind the pickup. Bullets streamed from the weapon like water from a tap and slammed into the truck.

Tito, like a startled cat, slid off the hood of the truck, just as fire from El Coco's Uzi shattered the rear window.

I counted three full seconds, knowing by the rate of fire that the Uzi would be out of ammo and, sure enough, the stream of bullets ceased.

I peeked around the bed of the truck in time to see him drop the mag and slam in another. I could also see that he was talking rapidly, as if to himself, but I knew that he wasn't. He was on the phone, calling for backup, no doubt.

And that bothered me more than the Uzi. I figured we had no more than two minutes before said backup arrived.

I ducked back behind the pickup, waited for a few seconds, then peeked out again, but Stern and El Coco were gone. I stood up and leaned back against our shattered car.

Bob appeared around the front of the car and said, "You good, boss?" as he swapped magazines.

"Yeah," I yelled, unnecessarily. But my ears were still ringing from the rifle fire in the car.

"I saw Coco and Stern," I said.

Bob nodded, as gunfire erupted again from beyond the Navigator. Someone was still putting up quite a fight.

"Tito is good?" I asked.

"Winged, but good," he replied. "Let's finish this."

I nodded, and we moved forward together around to the front of the pickup, rifles at the ready. As we cleared the truck, we could see the second truck beyond the SUV. It was turned slightly in the road and El Coco, Henry Stern, and three more soldiers were using it as cover, exchanging fire with TJ and Tony.

Bob and I took aim. We both knew to not shoot El Coco or my lookalike and, two seconds later, the three soldiers lay dead at his feet.

El Coco spun around, the Uzi hanging from his right hand at his side, its magazine empty, and he smiled.

"You two are coming with us, now," I shouted.

Rickey *"El Coco"* Mendoza merely shook his head, still smiling.

It was then that I heard the sirens.

Bob and I craned our necks and, in the distance, I could see three dark blue and white pickups racing toward us.

The police? For just a few seconds I felt relieved. They'd arrest El Coco and keep the Carbena backup at bay.

Er, no. They wouldn't, I realized as I remembered that military riverboat.

I heard Tito yell something in Spanish I didn't understand, but my gut was telling me it was a curse.

A split second later, a soldier standing in the bed of the front blue and white truck opened fire.

I saw Tito running and returning fire.

"We gotta get out of here!" Bob yelled.

We had just seconds before the police would overtake us.

TJ and Tony, somewhere out of sight, opened fire on the police truck, peppering it with bullets. Its right front tire collapsed. The truck lurched into a sharp turn to the right. Its front wheel bit into the pavement, and the vehicle rolled, slamming into a parked car.

I watched as the cartel boss, my lookalike at his side, strolled casually, smiling, around their own shattered pickup.

Tony's car somehow whipped around and, burning rubber, they sped away, TJ and Tito firing from the windows.

Bob and I ran back to our car, and I knew right away it was a nonstarter, literally.

"C'mon. We gotta run for it!" Bob yelled.

And we did, ditching our rifles as we went. We raced around a corner, into a narrow side street, pulled out our handguns and then broke into a flat-out run.

I glanced back over my shoulder, certain there would be a small army pursuing us. There was no one. When we came to the next corner, however, things changed, and not for the better. A pickup with *Policia Estatal de Tamaulipas* painted on the hood was rushing toward us. The uniformed officer in the truck bed had his rifle leveled... at us.

I raised my weapon, but Bob was even quicker. He squeezed off three shots, forcing the police officer to drop down below the back of the cab, a spray of blood erupting from his shoulder.

Again, we broke into a run, crossing the street, Bob leading, leaping up a wall that was six inches higher than he was, and over it.

I threw myself at the top of the wall, grunted as my fingers found purchase, and hauled myself up and over.

Oh geez. I'm getting too old for this crap.

Bob was waiting on the other side. We were in someone's yard. An old man in a metal rocking chair under a lean-to porch, nursing an Indio beer, stared at us with glassy red eyes.

I nodded to him as we ran past, through the backyard, over another much lower brick wall, and out into the street... just as another police truck pulled up and the officer in the front passenger seat fired at us. And we ran, chips of brick exploding from the wall behind us.

We sprinted for maybe twenty yards, then hopped over the wall into another, much smaller backyard, ducking under the clothes hanging on a line where an old woman was pinning a dripping pair of shorts. She looked at us in surprise, dropped the shorts and held up her arms.

We jumped over another dividing wall into another backyard at the rear of what was obviously an abandoned house. We raced around the house as shouting echoed from the yard we'd just left and out into the street.

A siren blurted at us, and we spun around as two more State Police trucks rushed toward us.

Me? I was gasping for breath, and I knew we were done for.

I stopped running, raised my hands and yelled for Bob to stop too. And then I heard more gunshots behind us. Bullets howled over our heads, and I watched as another clipped the arm of the police officer in the passenger seat of the lead truck.

I turned, elated, expecting to see Tony's car, and already thankful for TJ's sharpshooting.

But it wasn't them. Three motorcycles came screaming toward us, each with two young men aboard, the passengers on the rear seats each armed with automatic weapons firing over the shoulder of the man in front of him.

They wore no helmets, and they looked exactly like the thugs that had taken me across the river: tattoos, jeans, black T-shirts and shaved heads.

To say I was confused... Well, you get the idea. Were these people Carbenas, too?

The officers returned fire... At least they tried to. But the motorcycles were agile and their gunmen efficient. As one of the bikes passed a truck, the driver lobbed something into the truck bed, and I knew in my gut what it was even before the explosion. It was a grenade.

The lead truck was now in flames. The explosion had flung the police officer spinning wildly out of the truck bed to land in a heap on the pavement, and he lay still.

The other truck spun out of control, knocking over a street sign, then it sped away, the officer in the truck bed shuddering under a hail of withering fire.

The bikes wheeled around and rumbled slowly, quietly to where we were standing. Bob dropped his gun and raised his hands, but I held onto mine. I had no idea what to expect, but if these thugs were going to take me, they weren't going to get me without a fight.

I'd also remembered what that kid, Tattoos, had said to me back on the bank of the Rio Grande. *If you get the chance to shoot yourself, take it.*

But, to my surprise, nothing happened. The bikes came to an idling stop. The thugs just sat there, waiting, smiling, saying nothing.

A few seconds later a car, a beat-up Toyota Corolla, arrived and the guy in the front passenger seat rolled down his window and motioned toward the back door.

"Get in, *gringos*."

Bob and I looked at each other. We were surrounded.

"Look, get in, or we leave you for the *Policia*. Your choice."

Bob nodded. We got in.

The car sped away, flanked by the motorcycles.

"I guess I should say thanks," I said, although I wasn't sure I'd still be thankful when we arrived at our destination.

"No problem. It's our pleasure, *gringos*. You are with the CDN, now."

Bob rubbed his temple and said, "Oh, no."

"What's the CDN?" I asked.

The guy in the front passenger seat turned around and grinned at me. He had a huge gap between his two front teeth.

"It means..." he said, drawing it out. "The Cartel del Norte, Homes."

I sat back in the seat and closed my eyes.

Oh great. Another cartel?

25

Tuesday, July 22, 2019

11am

The hot afternoon air blasted through the open windows as the little car sped along the roads, making quick turns seemingly at random. I'm generally pretty good with directions. A lot of guys pride themselves on that. But this city gave me a headache. I had no idea where they were taking us. One minute, we were in what looked like an affluent neighborhood, and the next, we were bouncing down a narrow dirt road bounded by half-built block houses, most of which were occupied despite the fact that they had tarps over them instead of roofs.

The best I could figure, we were making our way to the western edge of the city, and that only because the sun, though high in the sky, was still behind us.

The terrain was arid, almost desert-like, with large cacti growing in the front yards. In downtown Nuevo Laredo, houses big and small were surrounded by strong walls. In this area, most had only flimsy wire fences.

Finally, after we'd been traveling for at least a half-hour, we turned onto a dirt road lined with houses in what obviously was a poor district.

There were large trees everywhere, in front of, behind and between the houses.

I glanced at Bob as we turned into one of the driveways and came to a stop. It certainly wasn't anything like I'd expected. While the Carbenas were holed up in a fortress as their local HQ, these people were using a small dwelling in a poor neighborhood, and there wasn't a mounted machine gun in sight.

The guy with the gap between his teeth got out and invited us to do the same. I stretched my legs and studied my surroundings.

Down the road, maybe a quarter mile, the two rows of houses gave way to a large field with soccer goals at either end. A dozen or so children were kicking a ball around, shouting and laughing.

Men, young and old, were seated outside dwellings, talking, smoking, drinking beer. Women were gathered in groups, talking together rapidly in Spanish. And it was hot, hot and dry. It was a poor section of the city, but it was also... quite peaceful, a window to a better time.

And then the paradisaical fantasy bubble I was in popped when a group of at least ten guys came around one of the houses, all dressed in full tactical gear: vests, military boots, knee guards, machine guns at the ready or slung around their shoulders, extra magazines in their utility belts. Several of them had bandanas either around their necks or over the lower half of their faces. They reminded me of the *banditos* of the old west.

In the middle of this small troop of cartel soldiers was a tall, heavyset man wearing cowboy boots, blue jeans, a colorful western-style shirt, a tan cowboy hat, and a gun belt with a pearl-handled, chrome-plated .44 Magnum revolver in the holster. His dark, lean features were accentuated by a neatly trimmed goatee, bushy eyebrows and a large smile. He had an air of authority about him and was obviously the man in charge of this local gang of desperados. He was an intimidating figure to be sure. Fortunately, though, he seemed to be in a good mood because he was smiling hugely.

Gap Tooth pointed at the large man and said, "That man is the Boss around here. His name is Franco de la Cruz, and he will decide if you are to live or die."

Well, with an introduction like that, I was sure as hell going to be on my best behavior, wasn't I?

Again, Bob and I exchanged glances and I wished I could ask him some questions, questions that had been burning in my brain the whole time we were on the road.

Who exactly are the CDN?

Why didn't he tell me there was another cartel in town?

What kind of reputation did this Franco de la Cruz have?

Gap Tooth and the driver of the Corolla gently pushed us toward the front of the car. Once there, the soldiers stepped forward, flanking us, walking around us, looking us over.

De la Cruz continued to smile. He pointed at me, wagging his finger, and said, "You! You look jus' like Henry Stern."

I had an instant flashback of Joe in the diner, so I put up my hands and said, "Sir, I can assure you, I'm not."

The man laughed out loud. He sounded like a... I don't know what he sounded like, but he didn't seem to be threatening.

"I know, I know. But you look like heem."

I heaved a sigh of relief.

"Your name," de la Cruz continued, his accent distinctly Texan, "is Harry Starke, and you come to us all the way from Tennessee. You are a wanted man, *señor* Starke. I got some bounty hunter buddies on the other side that would love to get their hands on you, my frien'."

He turned to Bob. "And you... You are one slippery *cabron*. Your exploits in the south are well known to me, *señor* Ryan. I thought you were dead."

Bob smirked at that but didn't reply.

De la Cruz nodded thoughtfully as we all just stared at one another for what seemed like an eternity.

Finally, de la Cruz lifted his hands, shrugged dramatically and said, "So, what am I to do with you, boys? I hear you *gueros* have been causing trouble for El Coco. I don' know why, but I hear you try to kill him or kidnap him, or, I don' know, bust his balls, and you don' invite Franco to the party?" He rubbed his chest, his face falling in mock sadness. "I'm hurt, Tennessee."

"We didn't mean to insult you, *señor*," Bob said. "We

were in a situation and needed El Coco... and Henry Stern."

Bob glanced at me, inviting me to continue the story.

"It's true," I said. "Those two have caused big trouble for me and my family. They're trying to frame me for killing a Texas Ranger. I need them to clear my name."

De la Cruz looked at me. He was no longer smiling, his face serious. "What you're doing is starting a war, Tennessee. You know how many of my boys are going to die because we saved your pale white asses today? How many businesses will be shot up or torched because Ricky is pissed off because you shot up his favorite set of fancy wheels?" He was practically spitting. "You Americans think you can jus' come across the border and wage war with *Los Carbenas* and then leave us to pick up the pieces? You know who will suffer because of your little vendetta with El Coco and his little blond monkey, Henry Stern?"

He pointed at a group of five small kids who were playing tag with a dog. "Them," he said, "and them." He pointed at several women carrying baskets of laundry home from the clotheslines. "And them," he said, finally, pointing at a family gathered under a tree, sitting on folding chairs, watching a movie on a tablet propped against the tree.

He looked back at us. "They will suffer. Their children and *sobrinos* will die, and then they will come to Franco for help. And I will help them. But I can't help everyone. How can I?"

I didn't know what to say to any of that. I figured, by the look of the soldiers and that .44 Magnum hanging from his belt, that I shouldn't say anything to make the man any more pissed off than he already was.

He stared at us each in turn, then turned away, waving at us dismissively. "Put them in the back. I have to think about what to do with them."

The soldiers grabbed us by the arms and pushed us forward. We didn't resist.

We were taken around the back of one of the houses and there, hidden among the trees, I saw what I'd thought was missing from the cartel hideout. Trucks. A long line of them covered with camo netting. There were two armored trucks, a couple of military Humvees, a dozen or so pickup trucks, some with mounted guns, and several Jeeps. Some were old. Some looked quite new. All of them had the same three letters painted on them in white: CDN.

They were well hidden, yes, but this cartel wasn't any less well armed than the Carbenas, at least as far as I could tell. In fact, these soldiers looked more professional, better trained and better armed, than Goatee and his thugs.

We were ushered into the back door of the house, then into a small room off the hallway. The room was unfurnished, except for a table and two chairs.

We were ordered to sit down, in Spanish, by the soldiers. And we did. And they left us, closing and locking the door behind them.

"Who the hell are these guys?" I asked when I was sure I wouldn't be heard.

"The Cartel del Norte is new," Bob replied. "They are local guys, I think. I don't know much about them."

"You're working on a way to get us out of here, I hope?"

"You bet I am, boss."

"Yeah, me too." It wasn't a lie, exactly. I didn't have a plan yet, but it wasn't from lack of trying.

We heard a scraping sound coming from outside, and then the door opened again.

A young man, probably not much older than Tim, came in carrying a large can of some kind of energy drink in one hand and dragging a metal chair behind him with the other. At least, I figured it was an energy drink, judging by the neon lettering and lightning bolt designs on the can.

The kid placed the chair against the wall, close to the door, facing us.

Then he sat down, pulled a gun from his waistband and laid it on his thigh. He opened his energy drink with a snap.

"I speak English," the kid said in a thick Hispanic accent. "I went to Harmon Hall. Franco paid for the classes."

"That's good," I said. "Your English is good."

"You stay in those chairs, and we can be friend', hokay?"

"Okay," I said.

"Sure," Bob agreed.

"But if you make a move toward the door..." The kid grabbed the gun with lightning speed, pointing it at Bob's chest, then swiveling it to mine. "...then we are not friend' no more. Hokay?"

I nodded. "Got it."

"Franco, he taught me to shoot, too. He say I'm the best shot in Nuevo Laredo. And the fastest. My hands, they are fast, right? So do not even think about doing something stupid."

I put my hands up, palms out. "Hey, I wouldn't think about it, would you, Bob?"

"Nope," Bob said.

"We want to be friends," I said, smiling.

The kid took another sip of his drink and looked at us. Then he reached into his pocket and took out a smartphone and a pair of wired earbuds. He stuffed the buds in his ears, fiddled with the phone, and in no time at all he was listening to American rap music so loud we could hear it from across the room.

And he watched us, his eyes never wavering, and I wasn't about to make his hand even twitch.

26

Tuesday, July 22, 2019

Afternoon

I estimated two hours must have passed as Bob and I sat together in that room waiting for something to happen.

The kid with the big ears and twitchy eyes... eyes that only got twitchier the more of the energy drink he sucked down his throat, bobbed along to the rap music, as if in a trance.

We both kept our eyes on the kid, mumbling back and forth to each other when we thought the kid wasn't watching. We both were convinced that, as long as his eyes were open, making a run, either for the door or the gun, was a bad idea.

Even if we could somehow out-run or out-smart the kid, and even if we could grab his gun, we'd both seen the well-trained soldiers outside. Based on the number of vehicles we'd seen hidden among the trees, I was sure there were a lot more than that original group that had greeted us. I figured it was likely that de la Cruz had a hundred, or more, men scattered around the neighborhood. To try anything would have been pointless, if not downright dangerous.

"You think this guy's going to kill us?" I whispered.

Bob said nothing for a long minute, thinking. "I don't think so. If that was his plan, he would have taken us out already. I'm thinking he's going to interrogate us."

I weighed that thought, sucking my teeth. "No, I don't think so, Bob. The more I think about it, the more I'm sure he genuinely doesn't know what to do with us. We're an anomaly, a wrench in his machine."

He shrugged and said, "Then why rescue us? It makes no sense."

"Maybe he's looking for an ally."

"You think? I wouldn't bank on it. This cartel might be new, but it's also deadly. You saw the soldiers and the trucks outside, right? I think Franco is gearing up for war. A savage, bloody war."

"So he needs allies," I said.

The kid's eyes twitched, darting back and forth between us.

I remained still. Said nothing.

After a minute more staring at us, the kid's head started bobbing up and down again in time with the music.

"I hear what you're saying," I continued. "And, yes, I saw the trucks. So, maybe you're right. Maybe de la Cruz is preparing for war. If so, it was going to happen anyway. So maybe we can persuade him to let us ride along and get our hands on Henry Stern."

Bob shook his head and was about to reply when the door opened. A thug came in and waved for the kid to follow him. He took out his earbuds, paused the music, looked hard at us and picked up his gun.

"I will be right back," he said. "Don' you move, hokay?"

"You got it," I said.

The kid smiled, stood up, turned and walked out, closing the door and locking it behind him.

For the first time since we were picked up by the CDN, we were truly alone.

We looked at each other.

Bob stared at me and said, "What do you want to do, boss?"

It would have been foolhardy to try anything, and we both knew it, but sometimes action, no matter how futile, is better than sitting on your hands.

"I don't know," I whispered quickly. "I think maybe it's a trap."

Bob nodded.

He just started to get up, maybe to check the door or look out the single small window when the door opened again.

Bob straightened and sat back down.

We stared as the kid walked back in, gun in hand, and I wondered if he'd noticed anything.

If he had, he didn't comment. He simply stood to one

side as a young woman, probably no older than twenty, followed him in carrying two plates of food.

"This is my sister," the kid said proudly. "She no speak English. I mean she does not speak English."

The girl looked nervous, eyeing us both, and then Bob in particular, as she set the plates down on the table. Then she blushed, turned away and mumbled something in Spanish to the kid.

The kid grinned at Bob and said, "She thinks you're sexy. She likes muscles."

The woman looked at him, obviously angry, and chattered something through gritted teeth.

Bob grinned. I'd seen that look many times before. Then he said something in Spanish to her.

She blushed dark red and hurried out of the room.

The kid stared at Bob and said, "*Hablas Espanol?*"

"*Si.*"

I looked back and forth between them.

The kid laughed. "You did not tell me."

The girl, still blushing, came back with two Styrofoam cups of a pink liquid. It looked like Kool-Aid. Not saying a word, she set the cups down and rushed out again.

"Eat up... friends. The food is good. Enjoy."

The kid sat back down on his chair and turned on his music.

I was kind of impressed. He must have been about twenty-five and his ability to keep his attention focused on the two of us for so long was remarkable, energy drink or no energy drink.

Bob and I scooted our chairs up to the table. The food

was good—beans and rice and some kind of chopped meat in a red-brown sauce, plus a stack of corn tortillas. I'd never eaten so many tortillas in my life.

We hadn't been eating for more than a minute or two when we heard shouting outside. Ten seconds later, the door burst open, and two soldiers came in and grabbed us.

The kid jumped up, his gun trained on us.

We didn't resist. It would have been futile to do so.

We were taken to the front yard where we'd first met de la Cruz and where now TJ, Tony, and Tito, their hands tied behind their backs, were being held by a half-dozen cartel soldiers. TJ and Tony's faces were badly bruised. They'd obviously been in a fight, and Tito's shirt was stained with blood, though the sleeve had been ripped off and his upper arm had been bandaged.

The soldiers were obviously upset about something. One of them walked around behind our three friends and slammed the butt of his rifle into the backs of their knees, forcing them to the ground.

Two minutes later, de la Cruz came stalking out of the house, the .44 Magnum in his hand, and he looked mad as hell.

Bob and I were held to one side, at gunpoint. At de la Cruz's appearance, the soldiers holding our friends all began talking and yelling at once, waving their weapons in the air.

"Let me guess," I said to Bob. "They found those three snooping around and now they want to kill us all."

"Your Spanish is improving, Harry."

"You think?"

I'd been hoping we could make de la Cruz an ally. Well, that idea, so it seemed, had suddenly gone flying out of the window.

De la Cruz held up his hand and the soldiers stopped yelling. He turned to us and waved for us to be brought forward. The soldiers standing behind TJ and the twins had the muzzles of their rifles pressed to the backs of their heads. Bob and I were roughly pushed to our knees and guns were pressed to the backs of our heads, too—an experience I hope you never have to endure.

I figured we had about thirty seconds left to live, unless we could convince the cartel leader not to order our executions.

They say that when you're about to die, your life flashes before your eyes. That didn't happen. Not to me anyway. Instead, I smiled to myself at the irony of it all. It really did seem kind of funny, the situation we were now in.

Shady would have laughed, I'm sure. He'd orchestrated an elaborate scheme, knowing he probably wouldn't live long enough to see it come to fruition. And then, after all that planning with his buddies the Carbenas, we were about to be executed by the Carbenas' enemies.

Come on, Harry. I thought. *You'd better come up with something fast if you want to get out of this alive.*

I cleared my head and focused on de la Cruz.

"Can I say something?" I said.

Franco turned his attention, and his rage-filled eyes, to me.

"What new story do you want to tell me now, *gringo*?

Are you going to deny these three *cerdos* are your friends?"

I shook my head. "No, I don't deny it. They are my friends. The American works for me."

De la Cruz took two steps closer to me, and suddenly I became very aware of that rather large revolver in his hand.

"You have one minute," he said. "Explain yourself."

"Okay, look, Mr..." *What the hell am I supposed to call him? Mr. de la Cruz? Mr. Cruz? Franco? Just call him Franco.*

"Okay, Franco. You should know that I'm not here by choice. The Carbenas kidnapped me in Laredo and brought me across the river, and I was only in Texas because I'd been framed for murdering a Texas Ranger. But I didn't. It was Henry Stern who gunned the man down in cold blood... while he was eating breakfast."

I glanced at Bob, then at TJ and the twins, and said, "Yes, these are my friends. They're helping me clear my name. We figured that if we can get our hands on Stern and turn him in at the border, that would be proof enough that he killed the Ranger."

I couldn't be sure, but it seemed that Franco's anger was waning, so I decided to take a chance.

"Look, Franco," I continued. "We know that you're planning a war with the Carbenas. I think you want them gone from Nuevo Laredo. If that's what you're planning, I suggest we work together. Let's say that me and my friends are... quite handy in a firefight... I think your soldiers are well-trained, but so are we. Probably even more so. TJ is a soldier of Vietnam. He was awarded the

Silver Star and two Purple Hearts. Bob Ryan here," I said and jerked my head in Bob's direction, then continued, "he, too, is a United States Marine, CIA and God only knows what else. Tito and Tony... they, too, were trained by the CIA. So, if we work together, maybe we all get what we want. What do you say?"

And that was it. I'd tried.

I figured one of two things would happen next. Either we'd just signed ourselves up for a cartel war in this Mexican border town, or Franco de la Cruz was going to blow my head off with that damn great gun of his. Either way, there was nothing more I could do.

I thought of Amanda and Jade. If I was seconds away from death, my last wish would have been to see them one last time. Kiss them both. Tell them I loved them. Ask them to tell my father that I was damn proud to be his son and that I hoped he was proud of me, too.

I pushed those thoughts away and de la Cruz and I locked eyes. Neither of us blinked. Then, finally, he sighed and turned away.

"*Déjame pensar en ello,*" he said.

I had no idea what that meant, but I figured it wasn't an order to execute us because the soldiers all remained still, and silent.

De la Cruz began pacing back and forth in front of us, turning his head, first one way then another. He walked away, far enough that I couldn't see him through the gathered crowd.

A full minute passed. I didn't even realize that I was holding my breath until my lungs began to burn.

Finally, he came back. The crowd, the soldiers... all

eyes were on him. That revolver was in his hand, hanging by his side as he walked right up to me.

"Stand up," he said, finality in his voice.

And I did.

He was a little shorter than me—not more than an inch—but his presence was enormous. He stared at me. Then, slowly, he slid the big weapon into its holster, put out his hand for me to shake and said, "You have yourself a deal, Tennessee."

I grabbed de la Cruz's hand, and we shook, gripped each other's hands hard, and I couldn't help but smile. For better or for worse, I knew I'd just made a deal with the devil.

27

Tuesday, July 22, 2019

Afternoon

Within minutes of my cutting the deal with Franco de la Cruz, the soldiers and the crowd had dispersed, and we were taken into the house and offered more food.

Bob and I declined. We'd already had more than enough, and I didn't feel like eating anyway, not after so close a brush with death. Tony, Tito, and TJ, however, scarfed down the meat and beans and rice as if they hadn't eaten for a week.

A young woman in a colorful skirt handed out more of the pink drink—it wasn't Kool-Aid. They called it Jamaica.

Tito took a deep swallow and said, appreciatively,

"Ha, that is so good. It is hibiscus tea. Good for the blood sugar."

A few minutes later, the kid with the big ears and the twitchy eyes came in and said to me, "Franco wants to talk to you alone, *señor*."

"Well... okay."

"You will follow me."

And I did.

We walked out of the house, through the rear entrance, behind the long row of houses, from one back-yard to another. There were no fences or walls.

"Who owns all these houses?" I asked the kid. And it occurred to me that I didn't know his name. But maybe that was for the better. It wouldn't hurt so bad if he died in the upcoming battle.

He looked sideways at me, puzzled. "What do you mean? People own the houses, and they live in them."

"But all of you," I said, "you are all the cartel? You live here, too?"

"*Sí*."

"And the people... they are okay with that?"

"Of course. We are their guests."

I had trouble imagining that. I mean, if someone just moved into my neighborhood and took over like that, I wouldn't have considered them guests at all.

"So, where does Franco live?"

The kid pointed ahead at the house on the other side of the road at the end of the street. "He lives there."

Franco's house was just a little larger and a little nicer than the rest of the houses, but not by much. It didn't have a wall or fence either, so it was difficult to know where one property ended and the next began. People wandered from one house to the next, in and out, coming and going, seemingly as they pleased. The house where Franco lived was no different, other than the two soldiers on the roof, their rifles at the ready.

The kid waved at one of the soldiers as we got closer. We didn't go inside. Instead, we walked around to the back of the house where we found de la Cruz, a yellow ball in his hand and a large German Shepherd at his side.

When the dog saw me, its hair rose on its back and it snarled. I stopped dead in my tracks as the beast began to inch forward, its teeth bared.

"*Oye, oye,*" Franco said to the dog. It immediately calmed down and dropped to its belly.

Franco looked at me, smiled and said, "I apologize. I had to run before. You get enough to eat?"

I nodded. "Yes. Thank you."

He nodded at the kid, who bowed slightly then turned away and left us, swaggering back around the house.

"I had to take care of some business, and now *Guardabosques* needs his exercise."

"I'm sorry?" I said.

"What are you sorry for, my friend... We are all friends now, are we not?"

"Yes, friends... I didn't understand. Your dog. He needs his exercise?"

"*Guardabosques?* Oh, *si.* Now I understand. In English it means ranger. His name is Ranger."

He threw the yellow ball across the yard and the dog

leaped up and charged after it, its legs a blur of brown and black.

"You were right, by the way," de la Cruz said.

"Right about what?"

"We are preparing for war. Well, war may not be the right word. We're planning a coup."

"Against El Coco?" I asked.

"*Si*," he replied, nodding.

"And, you have a plan?"

Ranger came rushing back, the ball in his mouth, and dropped it at de la Cruz's feet, then stepped back and looked up at him, expectantly.

"There can be only one top dog, only one leader of the pack, right?"

I nodded. "Right."

Franco threw the ball again and Ranger took off like a bullet. *Geez, I wouldn't want that sucker after me.*

"Well, Cartel del Norte is ready to take that position."

I nodded along, trying to read between the lines, trying to figure out what he wasn't saying.

He shot me a look and said, "You have not heard of us, have you?"

"No sir, I'm afraid I haven't."

He smiled. "Don' worry, my friend. No one has."

Ranger came back with the ball, and Franco threw it again.

"You see, we are local. Almost all of the CDN comes from right here, from Nuevo Laredo."

"I figured it must be something like that," I said. "I

don't know much Spanish, but I do know enough to know that Norte means north."

He nodded encouragingly. "That is right. The Carbenas are thugs. They come from Tampico and San Luis and the far south. They don' care about these people. They do extortion and kidnapping. They kill anyone that looks at them... funny. They terrorize this city and other cities like it."

"And you don't?" I asked.

I watched his face, looking to see if he'd taken what I said as a challenge. Thankfully, he hadn't. He just grabbed the ball and threw it again. This time, the ball bounced clear across the large, open yard and out into the thick bushes and trees beyond.

"We treat our people well. We treat our city with respect. Look around you, Tennessee, and tell me, what do you see?"

I glanced around. I knew what he was getting at. People were going about their business, seemingly without a care in the world.

"Well," I said, "everyone is happy."

"Exactly. These people are under my protection. We share what we have. We give back to the community. You understand, *amigo*?"

I thought back to Franco's speech he'd made just a few hours ago, about how concerned he was that the people might be hurt or killed in a confrontation with El Coco.

"Okay," I said, "I understand. So how d'you plan to bring about the coup? How do you plan to take out the Carbenas?"

He pointed a thick finger at me and said, "One more thing you have to remember, Tennessee, is that most of them are not Carbenas. They are like us. They are locals doing a job. The boy on the corner, he don' care who he works for. They just do their jobs so they can earn some pesos for their family."

"I see," I said, starting to catch his drift. "So your war isn't with them."

"*Si*. They work for Los Carbenas. They worked for Los Zitas before that and for Del Golfo before that. And, when we take over, they will gladly work for us."

"So, what you're saying is that if you want to change the direction of the bus," I said, "you change the driver. The kids don't care which way they go."

Franco laughed. "Yes. And neither does the bus. It just goes. So we take out El Coco and his top lieutenants, and everyone else just goes back to work."

"So what exactly is the plan?" I asked, feeling like we were talking in circles.

Ranger came running out from the bushes, the ball in his mouth. De la Cruz grabbed it, eyed the dog. He was breathing hard, his tongue hanging out.

"That is enough for today, I think, *perrito. Acuéstate!* Ranger dropped to the ground and looked up at his master.

De la Cruz looked back at me and shrugged. "My men are working on a plan. We had one, but I think you and your friends have ruined it, *amigo,* so now we have to start all over again."

I frowned. "How did we ruin it, Franco?"

"You came close enough to Ricky Mendoza to kill

him. You scared him. He will not be sleeping in the same house tonight. He may even go into hiding. We have to find where he is before we can do anything."

I nodded and said, "I'm sorry."

And I was. I had no idea what we were getting into when we attacked his convoy, but then again, as I'd told Franco earlier, I didn't ask for any of it.

"So now you will tell me the truth, Tennessee. No bullsheet, got it? You got other people in this city? If so, we need to bring them here where they will be safe, especially after the... how you say? The stunt you pulled this morning. All of Nuevo Laredo will feel El Coco's wrath today."

Oh crap. Jacque and Tim must be worried sick about us.

I pulled my burner phone out. "I do, Franco. There are two more, but they're civilians, you understand?"

Franco nodded, turned and waved at the kid, who hadn't gone farther than the corner of the house, just out of earshot.

The kid ran to de la Cruz, who rattled off something in Spanish to him, then he turned to me and said, "He will go get your people. He can take one of your soldiers, so they will know they can trust him."

I looked at the kid and said, "Take Bob. He's the big one, the one your sister likes. Bob will take you to them."

The kid grinned, nodded, and ran off.

Franco shot me a comical look. "Little Ana likes your friend with the muscles?"

I didn't answer. I was calling Jacque.

"Harry?" she answered on the first ring. "Oh my God. Are you all right?"

"Hey Jacque. Yes, we're fine. I need you to listen to me and not talk. I have no more than a minute, okay?"

"So talk," she replied. "You're on speaker."

I spent the next sixty seconds or so explaining that Bob and the kid were on their way to pick them up and that they were to pack everything up and be ready when they arrived. I also gave a quick briefing about our new alliance and what we were about to do. Then I told her I had to go.

"Wait," she said. "Tim needs to talk to you."

"If we're going to be attacking these guys," Tim said, "we'll need more equipment. I wish I had my drone."

I looked at de la Cruz, who was patiently waiting. "What kind of equipment do you have? Computers, communications, that kind of thing?"

He unclipped a walkie-talkie from his belt, put it to his mouth, thumbed the key and said, "*Nacho, nacho, nacho, por favor.*"

Less than thirty seconds later, a thin young man with a shaved head and thick, hipster glasses came running out of the back of Franco's house. He was wearing a T-shirt with the image and logo of a rock band I'd never heard of.

Franco turned back to me. "This is Ignacio, Nacho for short. Nacho Reyes. He is our computer... geek? He speaks good English."

"Here," I said, handing the phone to Nacho. "Talk to Tim."

Nacho took the phone from me, and he and Tim soon were embroiled in a lively conversation.

"Yes, I have that," Nacho said. "That too... No, but we'll get one. Yes, low frequency but high range. No, the fidelity is higher than that. Well, it depends on how you wire it up."

De la Cruz laughed. "They will have even more fun when we are all together this evening."

"Right," I said. "Then we talk about the plan?"

Again, the cartel leader laughed. "No, Tennessee. It is Sunday. Tonight is fiesta."

28

Tuesday, July 22, 2019

Early evening

It was more than an hour later when Bob and the kid returned with Jacque and Tim. By then, the safe house we'd been held in had been thoroughly cleaned out and we were led by the kid's sister to a larger house, which didn't seem to have anyone living in it. It was clean and there were bedrooms and beds for everybody. Several of the rooms even had small window air-conditioning units that helped keep the house cool. But oh, how hot it was outside. I understood then how important the trees that surrounded most of the tiny houses were. Without their shade, the structures would have been little more than ovens.

And the hotter it became, the fewer people I saw walking around outside. It was siesta time in the cartel neighborhood. By four o'clock, even the soccer field at the end of the street was deserted.

The kid's sister brought us a change of clothes, most of which seemed to fit okay. I had no idea whose clothes they were or where they came from, but I was thankful for them anyway.

We took turns showering and then we also took time out to rest. I was surprised the CDN soldiers left us alone in the house.

It was around five o'clock when I gathered everyone together and proceeded to catch them up on what the cartel leader planned to do, that he planned to replace the Carbenas with his own outfit.

"We have to be careful, Harry," Bob said. "Changing cartels will destabilize the entire area. You want to be responsible for that?"

"I don't think so," TJ said. "From what I understand, this Franco guy's been planning this attack a long time, long before we arrived, right?"

"That's right," I said.

Jacque looked at me and said, "I'm with you, Harry. Whatever you decide is good with me. If this is how we clear your name, then so be it."

I glanced at Tim. He was nodding in agreement.

"Okay," I said. "So we stay safe and do what we have to do. Besides, I have a feeling de la Cruz will be a lot better for the community than the Carbenas."

"It always seems that way," Tony said. "And then..." He finished the sentence with a shrug.

"Tony is right," Tito said. "We will see their true colors when they have been in power for a while."

I wasn't going to argue with that. After all, the twins were Mexicans. They'd seen it all before, more than once, no doubt. And a part of me suspected they were right. The Carbenas weren't a local organization. Once they were gone, someone would want to march in and take the territory from the CDN for themselves.

The more I thought about it, the surer I became that this little coup, as de la Cruz called it, would lead to a long and bloody war between the cartels. Hopefully, we'd be long gone ourselves before that happened though.

I called a halt and told everyone to get some rest before dinner. I had a feeling it was going to be a long night, and then I switched the SIM again and called Amanda.

"Harry? Are you safe? Are you all right?" she asked as soon as she picked up.

"Yes, we're all safe. How about you? How's Jade?"

"Jade's doing fine, as you might expect—Maria is here —and yes, I'm safe, your father, too. When is all this going to end, Harry? I miss you so much. D'you have any news?"

"We're getting close, I think. We have a lead on Henry Stern."

I decided not to tell her the details. There was no reason to worry her any more than I had to.

"Speaking of your lookalike," Amanda said, "your father's managed to convince the police to look into him, and apparently they are. That has to help your case, right?"

"It might, but it doesn't mean I'm in the clear. They still have to arrest him for that Texas Ranger's murder, and they'll still need some kind of hard proof that I was framed."

I thought about how thorough the framing was, the plane tickets, the car rental and... the video. That kind of evidence is hard to ignore.

Truth be told, I was much more likely to prove I was innocent from Mexico than I was from a prison cell in Texas.

"I'm afraid the cards are still stacked against us, honey," I said. "Shady really did a number on me this time."

"Harry, stop it. I don't want to hear you talk that way, not now, not ever."

I opened my mouth to speak, but she just carried on, barely taking a breath.

"You're Harry Starke. You saved Chattanooga from a nuclear attack, remember? You've taken on small cases and big ones, and you've always come out on top, not because you're lucky or better than everyone else, but because you never give up. You do what you have to do, right?"

"I... guess."

"So, that's what you're going to do now. You're going to prove that you're innocent, and you're going to do it without breaking any *US* laws."

She emphasized the word *US* slightly, and I got her drift. I was going to do what I had to do in Mexico, but I had to stay clean, at least in the eyes of US law enforcement.

"You got it," I said. "Look, I have to go. I'm sure they've tapped your phone and will be trying to trace the

call. You stay safe, okay? Give Jade a hug and a kiss for
me. Tell my father I'm okay. I love you, Amanda."

"I will, and I love you, too, Harry."

I could hear someone talking in the background.

"Oh, and Kate says you better bring Jacque and Tim
back in one piece. TJ, too. Kate's quite fond of him, you
know."

"I know, and I will," I said, then told her to report this
conversation to the police right away. It didn't matter if
they were already tracing and recording the conversation.
The last thing I wanted was for some over-zealous DA to
arrest her on a bogus accessory charge.

We said our goodbyes and I terminated the call, took
the chip out of the phone and went out for a walk around
the neighborhood.

The sun was setting, but there was no letup in the
oppressive heat. In fact, it seemed to be getting warmer as
the sun went down. The people didn't seem to mind
though. Children played in the street, some wearing flip-
flops, most barefoot. Men outside the tiny houses were
washing their cars and trucks, drinking Tecate and
singing along to Spanish songs on the radio.

In the field next to Franco's house, some of his men
were wheeling grills from their yards and placing them
end to end in a long line. A pickup arrived filled with
wood and bags of charcoal.

I walked to the edge of the field and watched them,
thinking about the day I was arrested. I'd been planning to
grill that evening. I discarded the thought. It was depressing,
and these guys were having fun, and the festive atmosphere

was contagious. One of them came over to me, grabbed my arm and rattled off something in Spanish I didn't understand. No matter, he hurried me across the field to the line of grills where a youngster speaking Spanglish informed me that I was to take charge of one of the grills. I smiled and did as I was asked. Someone shoved a can of beer into my hand. Smoke billowed up from the line of grills. From a distance, it must have looked as if a house was on fire.

Then, two more pickup trucks arrived, their beds packed with huge red and white coolers. Three of the coolers were filled with meat, thick, juicy steaks and strips of paper-thin *carne*, all seasoned, marinated and ready for the grills. The rest of the coolers were packed with ice and beer.

Franco, as always, was in charge of the festivities. His hearty laugh could be heard from one end of the field to the other as he went from grill to grill, inspecting the charcoal. Only he could determine if a grill was ready to start cooking meat. When a grill was ready to go, he'd slap the man attending the grill on the back, howling in laughter and celebration.

"Ah, I see you know your way around a grill, Tennessee," he said.

"Hey, we have grills in the US," I said.

"I know that, *amigo*. I was in Houston for a while, you know."

"Really?"

I wanted to ask him about it, but, before I could, Franco slapped me on the shoulder and moved on to the next grill.

And so the long day came to an end, and night fell to the sounds of music playing on an assortment of radios.

Bob, TJ, and the twins arrived, then Jacque and Tim, and they gathered around to see what I was doing. I grinned at them and waved my tongs in time with the music. I have to admit that, considering the heavy cloud that was hanging over my head, I was feeling pretty good.

When the locals spotted Bob and the others, several of them ran to find folding chairs for their guests to sit in and soon they were seated, laughing together and drinking beer. It was a good time; one I would never forget.

The music grew louder. A small TV wired to a car battery was placed on a folding chair, and the men gathered around it to watch an important soccer match, hooting and hollering.

As night fell, more of Franco's men, on motorcycles, arrived and gathered around the tables where women were serving paper plates heaped with meat and rice and tortillas.

And then even more soldiers arrived. Truckloads of them came rolling in, all wearing body armor and guns slung around their shoulders. These men were a different breed, quiet, serious, unsmiling. They simply took off their bandanas and ski masks and ate in silence.

TJ strolled over to me, plate in hand, chewing as he walked. I had a plate of food and ate while I kept an eye on my grill.

"I count fifty-six trained men," he said. "That's more than I expected."

"Me too, TJ," I said. "Me too."

29

Wednesday, July 23, 2019

Morning

I slept well that night and was up early the next morning. All was quiet. No one was stirring and, knowing them, they probably wouldn't for at least an hour, so I decided to go for a run.

When I opened the door, the air hit me like a slap in the face. The sun wasn't even up, but it seemed warmer than it had when we finally went to bed last night. As I crossed the front yard of the house and, once outside, I realized why. The sky, barely visible in the pre-dawn, was thick with clouds that held the heat like a blanket. Beads of sweat began to form on my forehead even before I'd crossed the front yard.

I jogged slowly to the field at the end of the road—the grills were gone and the trash had been cleaned up—and that's when I noticed a familiar figure running smoothly around the field at a steady pace.

I watched as he ran toward me and finally stopped in front of me, breathing easily.

"So, boss, you're finally up," Bob said. "I thought you were going to sleep in. You coming?" And with that he turned and ran on. I ran after him and fell into step beside him.

The minutes slipped by and it wasn't long before I felt the energy return to my muscles and joints.

There was a time, before all that mess with the Iranians and the bomb, that a morning run was part of my daily routine, but I have to admit that I'd let things slip, those last several months, and I was decidedly out of shape. And, running alongside Bob that morning only reinforced the need to do better. He glided effortlessly along, breathing easily while I... well, let's not talk about the details. Bob was a powerhouse, his legs and arms moving like well-oiled pistons while I found myself struggling to keep up. To be honest, I was ashamed of myself and made myself a promise, right then and there, that I was determined to do better, if ever I could get myself out of the mess I was in.

We'd been around the field three times when Bob decided he was going back to the house to do some push-ups and then hit the shower. I told him to go on and then ran on, not because I wanted to, but because I was too embarrassed to stop. I went two more times around the field, and then I, too, headed to the shower, my lungs and legs on fire. *No damn push-ups for me.*

I hit the shower and let the cool water wash away the

sweat and the ill feelings I'd managed to generate for myself over my general lack of fitness, and again I made myself a promise to get back in shape.

I dressed in borrowed jeans and a T-shirt and then went into the kitchen to find that the neighbors had brought breakfast and a huge pot of coffee. Jacque was seated at the table nursing the first cup of the day. I poured a cup for myself and sat down beside her.

"Good morning, Harry. Good run?"

"Not so much," I said. "I'm so out of shape I can barely walk. I'm going to have to do something about that."

"Maybe we can have a gym at the new offices," she said, looking at me over the rim of her cup.

"New offices...? Yes, that's a great idea, if..." I looked at the food. "Do these people ever stop eating?"

She smiled and shrugged.

The twins came in, both showered and dressed.

"Ah ha," Tito said. "Tacos."

He loaded a plate and sat down. I looked at his food and was surprised to see that the tacos had different fillings. Some had eggs with green sauce. Some had eggs and red sauce. Others had potatoes and some kind of meat. Some had green vegetables I'd never seen before, chopped up and mixed with ground meat. Others just had beans.

Tito had grabbed two of each and started in on them as if he was starving. Tony opted for a piece of sugar-coated bread.

Me? I passed, but I have to admit, the tacos looked tempting, and any other time I might have tried one or

two with my coffee. But after my performance earlier...
Well, you get the idea.

By eight o'clock that morning everyone was sitting
around the table, eating and joking and drinking coffee...
Well, almost everyone.

"Where's Tim?" I asked.

Jacque waved her hand and said, "Oh, he and that
Nacho guy went off together earlier, chattering about
computer stuff."

We'd all just about finished eating when Franco and
two of his men joined us. We made room for them at the
table, and they sat down, their faces serious.

"We know where El Coco is," Franco said. "It is time
for us to make a plan."

One of the two guys with Franco was the kid with the
big ears and a penchant for energy drinks. He was so
young that I was surprised he was in on the planning.

The other guy with Franco was older, with short-
cropped white hair and glasses. He was wearing body
armor, black jeans and T-shirt. He was obviously one of
the CDN soldiers. He looked around the table and spoke
in quiet, clipped Spanish. He finished what he had to say,
then Franco translated.

"El Coco is in the jail. He's scared that something is
going to happen, so he's gone to the most secure place he
knows."

I thought back to what I'd seen on Google Maps.
That jail was supposed to be a super-fortress controlled
by the Carbenas.

"That's not good," Bob said. "Security there is tight,
right?"

Franco nodded. "It is like the White House."

The older guy spoke again and took an iPad from inside his vest. I understood little of what he said, but I could tell he was smart and obviously a professional.

"The good news is," Franco loosely translated, "we have some people on the inside, some prisoners who have already pledged their loyalty to the CDN, people who are willing to help with an attack."

"What kind of help?" TJ asked.

Franco translated the question to the older man, and he answered.

"They will open the gate at the back of the jail," Franco said.

The soldier put the iPad on the table. He'd brought up a map of something I didn't recognize.

"That's not the jail, is it?" I asked.

Franco smiled. "No, it is the ancient island city of Tyre."

The old soldier pointed to the walls of the city, and the X's marked around the perimeter.

"When Alexander the Great conquered Tyre, he built a bridge from the mainland to the island. But he also used ships. He attacked from all sides."

The soldier pointed to one X that was bigger than the rest.

"But here," Franco continued, "is where they finally broke through the wall and soldiers were able to fight their way inside."

The soldier moved his finger around the map, describing a circle around the city, the flow of Spanish unceasing.

"But the attacking ships had to continue to keep the city's defenses occupied. That way the soldiers at the break in the wall could successfully get inside and defeat the defenders."

"But what does any of this have to do with the jail?" Tony asked.

"I can answer that," I said. "If Franco's contacts inside the jail can open the gates, we can get some trucks inside and attack from behind. We'll still be outnumbered. So Franco wants to keep some of his soldiers on the outside, attacking the walls, to keep the Carbenas busy. Meanwhile, we go in hard and fast. We get in and we get out before they know what hit them."

Franco was translating as I spoke, and the older man looked at me and nodded solemnly.

"Well," Bob said, "you certainly have the numbers to keep up the external attack. It might work."

The kid leaned forward and said, "And the bike teams, they will be there too. We will delay the backup from arriving too quickly."

"Okay," I said. "It sounds like we have a plan. But what about the authorities? They came to El Coco's aid when we attacked his convoy."

"*Si*, that is true," Franco said. "But remember what I told you about the school bus?"

"Yes?"

"Well, the police and the military are just the kids on the bus."

I frowned. "I don't follow."

"Look at it this way. The police are not loyal to the

Carbenas. They are either bribed or threatened into compliance. They hate El Coco as much as we do."

"So you kill El Coco," Bob added in, "and the police won't care?"

Franco smiled. "More than that, *mi amigo*. They only care about who keeps the peace. They only care about who will be paying them off. If we are in control, they will be on our side. That is why we must hit the jail hard and fast. If we take this to a full-scale war, the authorities will not be happy. But if the fighting is over quickly, and we are successful... then they will fall in line."

I leaned back, thinking about it. "Sounds good to me. How can we help? On the inside, I assume."

Franco nodded. "*Sí*. You can do a lot to help us get in fast."

"Not Jacque and Tim," I said. "I want them away from the fighting."

Jacque shot me a dirty look, but she didn't protest.

"That will be okay," the kid said. "Tim and Nacho already gave us their list."

"What list?" I asked.

"*Sí,*" Franco said. "They say we have to have a drone to pull this off. They are certain of it."

I rolled my eyes. I was used to Tim asking me for new toys, but now he was turning his "wish list" in to a cartel boss? All I could do was shake my head and smile.

Franco laughed. "Do not worry, Tennessee. We have already purchased all of the best equipment. It will arrive later today. Nacho and Tim, they will be in a van near the attack, controlling the drone and... other things I don't completely understand. I believe Miss Jacque will be good with them. Nacho needs adult supervision."

Jacque nodded. "So does Tim, sometimes. I'll stay with them. I can drive the van."

I nodded. "Well, it looks like we have a plan."

"When do we start?" Bob asked.

Franco conversed quietly with his soldier companion. Finally, he turned back to us and said, "They will need the day to get messages to our supporters inside the jail. We think the best time will be early tomorrow, just before dawn."

"I like it," TJ said. "Dawn is always a good time to attack, even in the rain."

"There will be no rain, my friend," Franco said, and cleared his throat. "But..." He looked at me warily. "There is one more thing we might need your help with."

"What's that?" I asked.

"If the police are not convinced right away that we have won the day, we might need for you to pose as hostages."

"Excuse me?" I said.

"Well, if we show you to be a hostage, someone the Carbenas have captured, it might convince the police to let us take power. We would threaten to expose the American prisoners to the world."

"Oh yeah, I get it," Bob said. "Things aren't exactly kosher between the US and Mexico right now, and seeing US citizens on the news as prisoners of a Mexican cartel... that would make things between our two nations a whole lot worse. Yeah, they might just go for that."

"*Exactamente*," Franco nodded. "If we promise to

release you quickly, and quietly, the governor would order the State Police to stand down."

"Geez," I said. "Okay, fine. Whatever you say." I didn't like it much, but then again, it wasn't exactly a lie. I had indeed been kidnapped by the Carbenas. "If that's what's needed, you can use me first."

Franco grinned. "Excellent. Then we have a plan. Today we prepare..."

"And tomorrow, we fight," I finished for him.

30

Wednesday, July 23, 2019

Mid-day

Franco and his men left and, within an hour, more soldiers arrived with bags full of tactical gear, handguns, automatic rifles, ammo, magazines, vests and so on, for all, including Jacque and Tim. Though their needs were minimal since they would be in the van.

Speaking of Tim, I wondered where he was, so I went to look for him. I found him and Nacho sitting together under a tree, comparing notes. On what I had no idea but, from the words I did understand, I figured they were discussing the merits of a video game.

"Hey, Tim," I said. "Franco tells me you have some new toys."

They both looked up at me, grinning, and Tim said, "That's right, Harry. The drone and the comms Mr. de la Cruz bought for us will be here later today, so we'll be looking out for you."

"Not for us," Nacho said. "For me. You just get to use it while you are here."

They both snickered.

"Okay, that's good," I said. "Really good." I knew exactly what it was like going into battle with Tim's eyes in the sky to guide me, and I knew I couldn't have been in better hands.

"Better than good," Tim said. "You're really going to like the model we picked out. It's military grade and has smart-tracking technology, like what we used when you took Shady down, but this one also has both regular *and* infrared cameras."

"It is cutting-edge stuff," Nacho added, nodding enthusiastically.

"Well, what does it do?" I asked.

"It can track people inside buildings, and because of its onboard software," Tim said, "it can keep track of up to twenty different targets, registering their unique heat signatures and movement patterns."

I nodded. "It sounds like that could be useful," I said, thoughtfully. "But how will you know which heat signatures belong to who? We need to be able to track El Coco and Henry Stern. How will you do that if you don't know their signatures?"

"Is good question," Nacho said. "You must point them out to us. We will tag them and tell the drone to track them. Once we tag a heat signature with a label, the drone will not lose that signature. We will always know exactly where they are, as we will always know where you are, even if we lose communication with you."

"Got it," I said, nodding. "That makes me feel a whole lot better." I wasn't kidding. Going into a dangerous situation blind was always a nightmare, but with Tim, and now Nacho looking after us... Well, it might just give us an edge.

There was little more that needed to be said, so I bid them farewell and headed across the street to watch some kids playing soccer. None of them spoke English, but I soon realized from their chatter and beckoning motions they were inviting me to join them. I resisted for a moment, but they were insistent, so I thought, *why the hell not?* And I did.

It wasn't a serious game. The kids didn't pick sides. They just kicked the ball around and took turns trying to score a goal. One kid, a little older than the others, was wearing a pair of expensive soccer shoes, white with bright green stripes on them. He was the goalie, and he was good, and managed to block almost every shot. Once or twice, he had to dive to catch or block the ball, much to the delight of the rest of the unruly players, causing them to hoot, holler and laugh.

One of the kids ran to me and pushed me toward the goal, which caused even more fun and crazy laughter. It seemed they wanted me to be the goalie. I tried to tell them that I wouldn't be any good at it, but they wouldn't take no for an answer.

So, after a minute of fruitless protesting, I ended up between the posts.

The first kid to come at me with the ball was the older one. I figured he was going left, but as I moved in to block him, he went right, tapping the ball with the inside of his heel and it sailed by me into the corner of the net.

The youngsters went wild, jumping up and down with glee.

I laughed and kicked the ball back out to them, and it became a melee. All of them, at least fifteen of them, boys and girls alike, kicked the ball back and forth, seemingly at random until a younger boy decided to try for a goal.

He tried the same feint as the older boy, but I was ready for him. He knocked the ball with his heel in a perfect imitation of the previous shot. I managed to kick the ball away... right back to the same kid who was now within a couple of yards from the goal. With the precision a pro would have been proud of, he slammed it into the back of the net and ran away, his arms in the air like he was David Beckham acknowledging the cheers of the adoring crowd; in this case his loudly cheering friends. I have to tell you, I just couldn't help but laugh at this pint-sized hero.

On it went. One after another the kids tried to get the ball past me. And, I'm embarrassed to admit that most of them did. No, I didn't give them a pass because they were kids. I did my best, my competitive spirit getting the better of me. If I could block the shot, I did, pumping my fists in victory, much to the delight of one and all.

Finally, a little girl took her turn. She couldn't have been older than six or seven. Her hair was long and wild, and as black as the night. Her eyes were the color of honey, and she locked eyes with me, a mischievous grin on her cherubic face. She was... beautiful, and I couldn't help but wonder what Jade would look like when she was her age. And I suddenly wanted to go home. I wanted to play soccer, or softball, or... golf, whatever, with Jade and watch her grow up.

Anyway, the little girl clumsily kicked at the ball and it bounced and bobbled toward me. I pretended to go for it but missed, and the ball rolled into the net.

Everyone knew I'd missed on purpose, even the girl, I supposed, but she grinned and jumped up and down in victory. I joined in her celebration, doing a little jumping dance of my own.

By then I'd had enough, so I said goodbye and walked off the field, accompanied by a half-dozen of the boys, all chattering and slapping me on the back. It had been an enjoyable thirty minutes and I felt the better for it. There's nothing quite like a bunch of happy kids to lift your spirits.

As I walked back across the street, I could see there was something going on at Franco's house, so I headed that way.

There were eight or ten soldiers present and some other rough-looking men I'd not seen before. *Cartel thugs?* I wondered.

What's this then?

As I drew closer, I could see there was a man at the center of the group, his hands bound behind his back, his face bruised, one eye swollen shut. A woman among the crowd was shouting at him, spitting in his face as the soldiers held her back, trying to calm her down.

Finally, Franco arrived, put up a hand and shouted something in Spanish, and immediately everyone quieted down. By then, I was standing at the edge of the crowd.

The man was pushed roughly forward and forced to his knees in front of Franco.

Franco asked questions. The man began to sob, obviously begging for his life. But Franco wasn't buying it, and everyone knew it and began backing away, creating a wide circle around Franco and the man.

Franco turned and asked questions of the crowd. A man spoke. I had no idea what he said, but then the woman shouted what could only have been curses at the man. Several more people in the crowd shouted comments, Franco turning to listen to each one in turn.

Franco shook his head. He looked saddened by what he heard, then turned again to face the prisoner and spoke to him, his voice low, almost... sorrowful.

"That man got drunk last night and tried to rape another cartel member's daughter," Bob whispered in my ear, startling me. "The angry woman is the girl's mother."

"Daughter?" I whispered back. "How old is she?" My thoughts went to that beautiful little girl out at the soccer field.

"Fifteen," Bob said. "The man swears he doesn't remember it and says he's very sorry."

"Which is it?" I asked. "He doesn't remember or he's sorry?"

"He's trying for both," Bob replied.

The man pleaded some more, and Franco spoke. I

didn't need a translator to know what would happen next. I could see the resignation in Franco's eyes.

Almost casually, he pulled the .44 Magnum from its holster. It was quick. The man didn't have a chance to beg or scream. Franco put the muzzle to his forehead and pulled the trigger.

That revolver roared and the back of the man's head exploded like a melon with a stick of dynamite buried in it. Tiny flecks of blood speckled Franco's snow-white shirt and face. The man fell backward onto the dirt; dead even before he hit the ground.

Franco wiped the barrel of his gun on his jeans and holstered it. He stood for a moment in silence, looking down at the body. The crowd, too, remained quiet. Then he spoke to the crowd. His voice loud, angry.

Bob translated, "This man was punished by the girl's family. They came to me for justice. This man sinned against us all. He sinned against the community. And, because he was one of my men, he sinned against the Cartel del Norte."

Everyone nodded in agreement.

"We are *not* Carbenas," Franco continued. "We are not animals. We do not act in this disgraceful way." He looked again at the body and said, "Take him away and bury him." Then he turned and the crowd parted to let him through, and he walked away.

I looked at Bob. He clamped his lips together, shook his head and said, "Let's go to the house." And we did.

Me? I was shocked, disturbed. Did the man try to force himself on a fifteen-year-old girl last night? I think he did, but still. Then again, I figured I needed this reminder that these people were a law unto themselves and wouldn't hesitate to deal out harsh and swift justice. And I knew now just how ruthless Franco de la Cruz was, and that if he saw me, or anyone on my team, as a threat, he'd kill us without hesitation.

31

Wednesday, July 23, 2019

Afternoon

The clouds above Nuevo Laredo that afternoon were thick and gray, a constant threat of rain, but not a drop fell. The atmosphere was oppressive, as much for what we'd just witnessed as for the weather.

I was in a mood to just sit around and wait... and mope, so I sat down with Jacque and her iPad and asked her to pull up Google Maps, and she did. It seemed the neighborhood was well-supplied with Wi-Fi.

"Since you're going to be driving the tech van for Tim and Nacho," I told her, "I want you to memorize the area around the jail as thoroughly as possible."

"You got it, Harry."

"If things go south tomorrow morning, we may need

to run for the border. If so, we'll need multiple escape routes. D'you think you can handle that?"

"Oh yeah. I can handle it," she said as she pinched and scrolled, studying the map. "Looks to me like there are three bridges over the Rio Grande in the area served by highways here, here and here." She pointed to them, each in turn.

"Oh, and Monterrey is a big city, only... two hours away? Maybe three. As a last resort we could head that way, then turn northeast and cross at Reynosa into McAllen, Texas. It would be a bit of a haul, but it's doable."

I nodded. "Okay. That's good. We have the option to go north or south. Bob seems to know this city quite well, too, but I don't like having all my eggs in one basket."

"It sure is nice having Bob with us again, isn't it, Harry?" she asked.

I nodded. It really was. I'd forgotten just how valuable he'd been in the past. And I missed his apish personality and unflagging sense of fun we'd all missed since he left.

"Speaking of the devil," I said. "Where is he? Come to that, where's everybody?"

Jacque shrugged. "Out, I guess."

"Okay. I'm going to leave you to it. Study that map. I don't want to get caught with my... I don't want to get caught napping. I'm going out for a while. See where the hell they all are."

I left Jacque to study the map. I didn't like not knowing where my own team was, especially in the midst of a cartel hangout.

As soon as I stepped outside, the oppressive heat smothered me. And yet there were people still walking the streets, most of them women and children.

I spotted Tim and Nacho walking toward Franco's house, their laptops tucked under their arms.

Bob was under a tree unabashedly flirting with the kid's sister, the same girl that had blushed yesterday when she got an eyeful of Bob's muscles.

Bob caught my eye and I frowned at him, albeit playfully. Bob was an adult, and he could do what he wanted. He'd come here to help me, and he certainly didn't have to. And, a lifelong bachelor, he was always on the lookout for a little romance. But I still had the image of the man getting his head blown off fresh in my mind. If Bob pissed off the wrong person, it could be him with his wrists bound, facing Franco's .44 Magnum, and that I couldn't have stood by and watched, which would mean a quick death for both of us.

"Harry," TJ said, appearing suddenly as if from nowhere. "Franco wants to take us on a drive. Apparently, we need some supplies."

I nodded to TJ and motioned at Bob. He whispered something to the girl, who giggled.

"You want to go for a ride?" I asked when he joined us. "See how the CDN operates?"

"Sure thing, boss."

TJ cracked a smile. "Apparently, I'm not allowed to call you that, Harry."

"Technically, neither is he," I said. "But he's never listened to me before, and now I don't sign his paychecks, so I have no leverage."

TJ led us to a line of four vehicles, two pickups and two Jeeps. Franco was standing by the nearest one.

"Good. You are here. I am happy to see you. Now you can see our organization in action. We have supplies coming from the US."

He motioned for us to hop into one of the Jeeps with a stone-faced cartel soldier behind the wheel. I got in the front while TJ and Bob jumped in the back.

A motorcycle pulled up beside the Jeep and the Kid smiled at me. I rolled down the window. He pulled his gun, twirled it like a gunman in a cowboy movie, put the barrel to his lips and blew. Then he winked, holstered the gun, revved his engine and let out the clutch, and we were off, a convoy of the four vehicles and six motorcycles. It was at that point I was overcome with a terrible feeling of impending doom.

We didn't head into the city, at least not any part of it I'd seen before. Instead, we drove from one deserted country road to the next, eventually coming out onto a two-lane highway, which we followed for a while before turning off again onto another unpaved road that led, as far as I could tell, to the middle of nowhere.

Eventually we came upon a semi-truck, an eighteen-wheeler, parked along the side of the road. The driver, an older man with an ample belly and wearing bright red basketball shorts and a white T-shirt, was waiting by the rear doors of the trailer.

Our convoy came to a halt beside the trailer, essentially blocking the road. Three of the bikers sped on ahead, checking to make sure no one was waiting to ambush us, and we all got out of our vehicles.

Franco shook hands with the truck driver, speaking to him in Spanish, then handed him a fat roll of American bills.

The side of the semi was painted in white and red, with the legend *Quinteiro* painted on both sides and the rear doors in big black letters.

"That's the name of a grocery store in town," Bob said. "They must get their supplies from the US. This truck has Texas plates. I wonder what the hell it's doing way out here? Nothing legal, I bet."

Two of Franco's soldiers opened the trailer doors and lowered the ramp. The inside was stacked with boxes, almost to the doors and the ceiling, all on wooden pallets, with a pallet jack in front. Several of the soldiers began unloading the stacks and setting them down on the dirt road, while others began stripping away the plastic wrap that held the boxes secure on the pallets.

The boxes were all labeled as containing cookies, chips and crackers, soup mix, bags of white rice and canned goods. In the middle of each stack, however, were more boxes, plain boxes. These the soldiers opened to reveal cases of ammunition, automatic weapons, grenades, and Semtex and C-4 plastic explosives.

"I knew it," I said, elbowing Bob aside.

"So that's how they get that stuff across the border," TJ said.

Hidden deep inside the third pallet was a large wooden case. Franco turned to look at me, smiling hugely as the soldiers lifted it carefully out.

"That is the drone," Franco said proudly. "It is top of the line. Military quality."

I nodded. "Tim has expensive tastes."

Franco laughed. "Do not worry, *mi amigo*. So does Nacho."

The weapons, ammo, and the drone were loaded into the backs of the Jeeps and hidden under blankets, while the boxes of snacks and foodstuffs were stacked neatly into the backs of the pickup trucks. Franco shook hands one more time with the truck driver, then, wiping his forehead with a small towel, he motioned for all of us to get back into our vehicles.

The convoy took a different route back to the neighborhood, passing along small side streets, through several neighborhoods that looked as poor as the one where we were staying, perhaps even poorer.

Every few blocks or so, the driver of the lead truck would sound the horn, and kids and families would come running out. Franco would jump down from the truck, pull several boxes from the back, open them and hand the food to the people.

Kids whooped and laughed. Mothers were moved to tears when they received bags of rice, cans of beans or soup packets.

Then Franco would jump back in the truck, and we'd move on to the next stop where he'd do it all again. It was no wonder to me why the Cartel del Norte was so popular with the people. Franco was their benefactor.

Finally, after driving around for so long that I'd lost any clue I might have had as to where we were, we turned a corner onto a dirt road that led back toward Franco's home neighborhood. And again, at the sound of the horn, women and children came running out of their homes and Franco distributed the remaining food.

I climbed down out of the Jeep and watched.

"I've seen this before," Bob said as he joined me, TJ at his side.

"You have?" I said.

"Oh yeah. Warlords all over the world do it, to gain the support of the people. It always works, until... they drop the hammer."

TJ nodded. "It's true," he said. "I've seen it too. All these gifts, all the generosity, it's for only one purpose; to buy loyalty."

"I understand," I said, thinking back to the way Franco had administered summary judgment to the attempted rapist that morning.

"They're generous now," Bob continued, "and the people love them for it, but then the generosity turns into cruelty, oppression. It's always the same."

I saw the little girl, the one I'd allowed to score a goal that morning. She was running, carrying a bag of rice, her little pink flip-flops slapping her heels as she ran to her mother, happy, like the rest of the kids.

But how many will live to see adulthood? I wondered. *How many will end up dead in a ditch, casualties of a long and bloody cartel war?* I suddenly felt sick to my stomach.

"We need to get out of here," I said.

TJ shot me a knowing look. "The sooner, the better. I agree."

Meanwhile, Franco continued to hand out boxes, like some Mexican Santa Claus, and they loved him for it. It was sickening.

32

Wednesday, July 23, 2019

Evening

I t was late in the afternoon that same day when I decided to call my father. August sounded tired.

How much stress has this put on him? When it's over... if it ever is, he deserves a vacation, my treat.

"It's good to hear from you, son. Are you safe?"

"I am, and, even better than that, I think there's a good chance I'll be home soon."

"That's good to hear. The sooner you turn yourself in, the better."

"I know, I know, and I will," I said. I knew he was giving me good advice, especially as he knew that law enforcement was listening to the conversation.

"It's actually better than you think," August said, "Raymundo has been working hard for you. The case against you is full of holes, and we're documenting every single weakness."

"Well that's good to hear," I said, surprised. I'd figured, after the deaths of two Laredo cops, no one would want to hear about how innocent I was.

August quickly filled me in on a few of the details. So many pieces of the puzzle were being exposed by Raymundo's team. Apparently, there was now proof that I hadn't purchased the plane tickets or rented the car from San Antonio to Laredo. The ballistics reports had definitely been tampered with, proving that my gun had not been involved in the drug-related execution several months earlier. I breathed a sigh of relief when I heard that.

"Son, I'm pretty certain you'll be fully exonerated if you turn yourself in."

"I appreciate that," I said. "I really do, and please thank Raymundo for me and tell him I'm sorry I was so... abrupt with him back in Laredo."

Wow, that feels like an eternity ago now.

"I will, Harry."

"But I can't come home yet. You see, clearing my name is only part of it. This lookalike of mine, this Henry Stern. He's here, in Mexico, and he works for one of the cartels, and as long as he's free I could be blamed for whatever criminal activity he might be involved in. I can't have that. He needs to be taken off the streets and tried for his crimes."

"I understand," August said.

"Thanks... And he killed a Texas Ranger. And then

there's those two Laredo cops. So you see, it's not just about me."

"Okay, son. Do what you have to do, but stay safe, you hear me?"

"I do. Look, I need to go. I'll be in touch."

I hung up and took the SIM card out of the phone, then went for a walk, thinking about how much was at stake on what was to happen the next morning. The enormity of what we were planning suddenly came home to me and I began to wonder if we were doing the right thing. In the end, though, I knew we had little choice but to go along with what suddenly seemed like a crazy plan. We were planning to break into a Mexican prison, for Pete's sake, and abduct or kill a crime lord protected by an army of... terrorists.

And so I walked the neighborhood from one end to the other and then back again. And it was hot, humid, so humid I could have been in a sauna.

As I approached the soccer field, I saw Tim and Nacho out there setting up the drone. It was massive, painted a matte black, with six propellers and two independently operated cameras. Jacque and TJ were at the edge of the field, away to my right, watching them.

The propellers were spinning. Nacho was holding a large and complicated-looking controller. Tim was staring down at a tablet.

Suddenly, the drone lifted slightly, then shot straight up, several hundred feet, its propellors barely making a whisper. *Wow! That thing is fast.*

Nacho and Tim were both laughing. But I knew they

weren't fooling around. They were testing the limits of their new equipment.

Where are the twins? I wondered. *I haven't seen them since this morning.*

"That's quite something, isn't it?" Bob said as he joined me.

"Yes, they really know their stuff... Makes me feel old, Bob."

"I hear ya, boss. I sometimes wonder if it's not time we hung up our guns and retired, sat back and enjoyed life, a little."

"You wouldn't know what to do with yourself," I said.

"Maybe you're right... Then again, maybe I'll surprise you."

I turned to look at him, smiling. He grinned back at me, tilted his head to one side and shrugged.

And then Franco arrived and we all gathered under the shade of a huge tree. Several of his soldiers joined us, including the humorless commander from earlier that morning.

"We must discuss the details of the plan," Franco said. "Your friend can translate, Tennessee?"

I looked at Bob. He nodded.

The short version went something like this: the trucks were divided into six groups. Two groups would launch an all-out attack at the front of the jail, which was on the east side of the complex. Two smaller groups would harass the north and south walls. They were to keep moving, firing at the guard towers. The idea was to keep the guards around the jail busy.

A fifth group would attack El Coco's yellow house,

about half a block from the jail. This was important because that fortress could provide backup to the jail.

The Kid and his bikers would patrol the entire area, keeping any incoming backup at bay and radioing in if danger was approaching from any direction.

All of the aforementioned was designed to create a diversion and as much chaos as possible, as quickly as possible, so the sixth and final group could infiltrate the jail. They'd go in through the rear gate at the western side of the facility, where they'd be joined by at least a couple dozen inmates. We were to be in that sixth group.

I leaned over and whispered in Bob's ear as he continued translating.

"They haven't said how many Carbenas are inside the jail, have they?"

"No, they haven't. I don't think they know for sure."

"Ah." I nodded.

"He did mention that there are Carbena kill squads all over the city."

"Looking for Franco?"

Bob grinned. "No. Looking for you."

Finally, Franco turned to me and Bob and switched to English. "And you will be entering the jail with us, correct?"

"I wouldn't have it any other way," I replied.

"Good," Franco said smiling, and then continued in Spanish.

"He says the Carbenas have reigned in this city for too long. They've killed enough innocent blood. They've kidnapped enough brothers and sons and husbands. It's time to end them and bring a time of peace to the people of Nuevo Laredo."

"Oh brother," I whispered. "This guy's full of it, isn't he?"

"He's passionate," Bob said.

Eventually, the meeting broke up, and Bob and I wandered back to where Tim and Nacho were still working the drone.

"By the way," I said, "where are the twins?"

Bob grinned. "I was wondering how long it would take for you to notice. They snuck off after the meeting this morning."

"Why? Are they ditching us?"

"Not hardly. No, they will be our plan B."

I raised my eyebrows. "Plan B?"

"Don't worry. They'll be nearby tomorrow in a car, armed and ready to come in and get us if things go south."

"Why didn't you tell me, Bob?"

"Oh come on, Harry. They don't work for you. Besides, I figured you'd like the plan. What if Franco decides we're expendable and we have to shoot our way out of there. If that happens—and I don't trust the son of a bitch—we're going to need some help. So, Tony and Tito will be standing by, just in case."

And suddenly I realized that was a real possibility.

"Okay, you're right. Good thinking, but we need to bring the rest of the team up to speed."

"You got it."

Bob dragged Tim away from the drone and I went looking for Jacque and TJ. I found them talking together under a tree. Five minutes later we were back at the house gathered around the kitchen table.

"Okay," I said. "Let's go through our roles, just to make sure we're all on the same page."

Jacque said, "I'll be driving the van. Tim and Nacho almost have it ready."

"And you studied the maps as I asked?"

"Of course I did, Harry. I can get us to one of the international bridges in just a few minutes. I've memorized alternative routes to all three, plus two options if we have to make a run for it to Monterrey."

"Okay good. Monterrey is one of the biggest cities in Mexico, right? So we'll be able to hide there, should the need arise."

I turned to Tim and said, "Will Nacho be okay if we have to deviate from the plan tomorrow? I know you two have really hit it off."

"Yeah, don't sweat it, Harry," Tim said. "He'll be cool."

"What about comms?" I asked.

"Oh, yes. We'll be all commed up, and I'll be watching everything from the drone."

I turned to TJ and Bob, heaved a sigh and said, "Meanwhile, the three of us go in with Franco and his top soldiers. The plan being to take the jail as quickly as possible."

TJ smiled that same, bloodthirsty smile I'd seen so many times before, and it worried me.

"Sounds like fun," he said.

"Bob, you want to explain about Tito and Tony?" I asked.

Bob told the rest of the team about where the twins would be.

It wasn't a perfect plan. It was dangerous, and it could go either of two ways. The Carbenas could easily overpower and kill us all; El Coco would not go down without a fight. Or we could win easily and Franco could turn on us. That was something I didn't even want to think about.

But, it was the best plan we had, and we had to stick with it.

There was no partying that night. No drinking. Instead, the entire neighborhood turned in early, conscious of the need for rest before the big day.

I took a shower. The water was warm. The heat inside the house was oppressive.

Sleep didn't come easily that night.

33

Thursday, July 24, 2019

Early morning

At about three in the morning, I heard someone moving around in the kitchen. I got up to find both Bob and TJ sitting at the table, carefully cleaning and checking their guns.

"There's coffee in the pot," Bob said.

I nodded, poured myself a cup and joined them at the table. I'd chosen a pair of CZ75 9mm semi-automatics and six magazines for the CZs—capacity seventeen rounds each—and an M4 carbine and two thirty-round mags for it from the pile of weapons Franco had delivered the previous day. Bob had a pair of .45 1911s. Why he chose those I had no idea. They are the devil to strip and reassemble. They do pack one hell of a punch though, and Bob is one of the best shots I've ever met.

I set the cup down on the table and went to my room to get the weapons. I stripped them, inspected them, nodded at the pristine condition they were in, reassembled them, loaded the six mags and loaded the two CZs. Then I racked the slides to load the chambers, set the safety and ejected the mags. I then replaced the two rounds I loaded into the chambers, reinserted the mags, set the weapons aside and picked up my cup. Next I started going carefully through my own equipment.

A few minutes later, Tim came in, dumped himself down at the table and opened his laptop. He tapped at the keys for a few minutes, muttering to himself and constantly adjusting his glasses with his forefinger. For almost five minutes we watched silently as his fingers flew over the keys. Then suddenly he stopped, froze, his hands on the keyboard, and slowly looked up.

"What?" he said.

No one answered. We all just sat there smiling at him.

He opened his mouth to speak, but before he could, Jacque walked in. It was three-thirty.

She made another pot of coffee, poured one for herself, looked around the table, nodded, set the cup down and went to fetch her own weapon, another CZ75. Then she, too, sat down at the table. It was getting kind of crowded.

"You ever fired one of those?" Bob asked.

"No," she answered, "but how different can it be?"

Bob just shook his head and said, "That thing has a two-and-a-half-pound trigger. It's light to the touch, so be careful."

She stared hard at him, then nodded and went about cleaning and loading it. And I hoped to hell she'd never have to use it.

I stood up and poured myself a second cup of coffee, took a sip, then turned and looked at Jacque, my eyebrows raised in question.

She smiled at me and said, "I needed it strong, to wake me up. Drink it. You'll be glad you did." And I did. And she was right, as always.

Tim did a quick comms check. Made sure everything was working as it should—I was sure Nacho was doing the same for Franco—and then he and Jacque left us to go to the van.

Half an hour later, at four o'clock, we were all outside and ready to go. We were all wearing tactical vests, even Tim. I had my handguns in a shoulder holster, one under each arm, and my M4 slung on my shoulder. Bob and TJ were similarly dressed and armed.

Soldiers were milling around everywhere, drinking coffee, smoking cigarettes and speaking softly among themselves. I couldn't understand a word of any of it.

The trucks and Jeeps were driven out of the woods from behind the houses. The mounted guns were checked and loaded. Grenades were clipped to the railings for easy access.

By four-thirty, the Kid arrived at the head of a dozen men, all of them mounted on motorcycles.

At four-forty-five exactly, Franco stepped out of his house and joined his officers. He was bare-chested, but not for long. A young soldier ran forward and strapped him into a tactical vest big enough to cover his belly. He was wearing his signature tan cowboy hat and .44 Magnum, along with its twin on his other hip, and there was a fire in his eyes. This was *his* moment.

"You wanna ride with me, Tennessee?" he asked, slapping me on the shoulder.

"Sure," I said, wishing I could have refused, as Bob and TJ were led to the Jeep that would follow behind us.

I was about to climb into the rear passenger seat of Franco's truck when I saw the tech van go by, Jacque at the wheel, flanked by two men on motorcycles. Tim and Nacho would arrive early in order to get in position in time to get the drone in the air.

I tapped the comm in my ear. "You hear me, Tim?" I whispered.

"Loud and clear, Harry," Tim said.

"Me, too," Jacque said.

"Bob, here."

"TJ, here."

I let out a long breath. *Good. At least we're all in contact with each other*, I thought as I climbed into the truck.

One by one the trucks and Jeeps drove past us into the night, one group after another. The leading groups would be the first to attack. We, our group, would go in last.

Finally, after what seemed like an eternity, the last armored vehicle in the fifth group lumbered by and the old soldier got in behind the wheel. Franco climbed in beside him. A young soldier—he couldn't have been more than eighteen—clambered in next to me, in the back, and three more soldiers climbed into the bed of the truck, one to man the fifty-caliber machine gun and two armed with M4 rifles.

And then, just like that, we were off.

Our little group, with our truck leading, drove out onto the bumpy, dirt road. The group ahead had already disappeared into the darkness.

The road twisted and turned until, finally, it came to a two-lane highway. We followed the road toward the bright lights of the city. I saw lights coming toward us and then heard the roar of motorcycles. Four of them drove past, did a U-turn and then came back and settled in beside us, two on either side. We had an escort, so it seemed.

Our driver had a walkie-talkie, and he and Franco listened intently to that same, strange sing-song code we heard that night on the rooftop as we listened in on El Coco. It sounded like, "Dale, dale, dale, dale."

Finally, our group turned off the highway and then immediately turned right down a small side street. We were in the city now, and I was able to see the tail end of the group up ahead.

I leaned forward. In the distance, up ahead, I could see what looked like an open field, and beyond that a long wall topped with bright lights. The jail.

The convoy in front of us, and the one in front of them, slowed and then halted. The drivers turned off their engines, and we waited; the quiet was, quite literally, deafening.

Two minutes later, Tim's voice in my ear startled me. "We're set up. The drone is in the air."

Then the silence was broken by the sound of sporadic automatic weapons fire.

What started as a few pops here and there turned into short bursts of staccato gunfire. Then came the explosions and then the steady tacca-tacca-tacca of a mounted machine gun.

And then, quite suddenly, all hell let loose and it became a full-blown war zone.

The old driver's radio erupted. Different speakers yelling different codes as the fighting intensified.

I heard the engines fire up, one after another down the line, and then Franco motioned for us to move up. The driver started the engine, pressed the gas pedal gently, and our convoy began to crawl forward, lights off, toward the rear of the jail.

"Harry," Tim said in my ear.

I pressed the comm button with the tip of my finger and said, "Yes. What is it, Tim?"

"We have night vision and full infrared. We're tracking everything. It's a sh... It's a storm out there."

"Yes, I can hear. Thanks, Tim," I said.

Franco turned in his seat to look at me, perhaps wondering if I'd have news for him.

"It's.... it's awful, Harry." I heard the shake in the kid's voice.

Sure, Tim had seen fighting before. He was there when my house was ambushed by Shady's thugs. He gave drone support when we stormed Shady's warehouse, but that was nothing compared to this. A few guys. Maybe a few dozen. But there had to be more than a hundred soldiers, on both sides, fighting and killing each other.

And then I was thankful that Tim and Jacque were at a safe distance. Watching through the lens of a drone was bad enough. At least they weren't in the middle of it.

"It's okay, Tim. Just focus on what you're doing and try not to think about it, okay?"

Try not to think about it? That's the best I can come up with? That kid's going to be scarred for life.

"Okay," Tim said shakily. "We have movement toward the back gate. I think it must be some of the prisoners. Oh God, they're fighting the two guards... The guards are down. They're beating him..."

I swallowed, hard. I hated that he had to see it.

"Is the gate open?" I asked, hoping to keep him focused. I really had Franco's attention, now, too.

"Yes," Tim said.

I nodded to Franco. He motioned the driver to move forward faster and told him to take it easy, that he didn't want to lose the element of surprise.

"Uh-oh, Harry," Tim said. "I think someone just tipped them off."

"What? How?" I said sharply. I motioned for Franco's attention.

"I see four men with guns moving toward the gate."

"Thanks, Tim." I looked at Franco and said, "We have to move, now. They're onto us."

Franco yelled something in Spanish and the driver hit the gas, hard.

34

Thursday, July 24, 2019

Dawn

Our truck rumbled over the crest of a slight hill, bucking like a wild bronco, throwing dust and dirt in all directions. I was surprised the guys in the bed of the truck managed to stay aboard, but they did.

Better than that, the soldier manning the mounted machine gun fired a long burst at the guard tower near the back gate, literally tearing it to pieces and killing both the guards.

Up ahead, three armed men ran to fill the gap between the open gates while two more heaved on the gate trying to close it.

Our driver floored the gas pedal and the heavy truck surged forward like a horse out of control.

The three men at the gate began to shoot at us. A bullet shattered the windshield. The soldiers on the back of our truck returned fire—two M4 carbines and the 50-cal' mounted gun. The huge rounds slammed into one of the guards whose chest exploded in a fine, red mist.

Our truck hit one of the gates, now halfway closed, smashing it open and sending the guard that had been pushing tumbling backwards.

I'd expected the truck to stop in the courtyard there, so the rest of the vehicles in our group could catch up, but we didn't do that. Instead, the truck plowed on at top speed, turning at a slight curve to the left until we were heading right for a wooden shack.

It was then I realized the driver had been hit. Franco realized it, too, and yanked the driver's leg off the accelerator.

I braced for impact as the truck plowed into the side of the building, the wooden planks bursting inward, splintering. The truck was stuck, half in and half out of the building.

"Harry," Tim shouted in my ear. "Are you okay? You're in that first truck, right?"

"I'm okay," I said as I opened the door, rolled out of the truck, and landed on my shoulder, hard.

I scrambled to my feet and looked around. Three guards were rounding my side of the building, their guns up, ready to fire.

Without thinking, I raised my M4 and opened fire, and not just me. One of our soldiers from the back of the truck was on the ground and shooting, too. A second soldier leaped to the ground, squatted, and he, too, began to shoot as more guards appeared from behind a nearby building.

I glanced up at the mounted gun and saw that the soldier who'd been operating it was actually strapped to the heavy weapon and had died horribly under the impact. The overhang of the roof had smashed into his chest, just below the throat. He was bent over backwards at an impossible angle. Blood dripped from his mouth. His eyes were wide and lifeless.

Holy shit! What a way to go.

To my right, the door to the wooden building opened. I raised my weapon, but something stopped me from pulling the trigger as... Franco de la Cruz walked out as if he didn't have a care in the world. He had a .44 Magnum in each hand which he casually raised and fired two rounds, hitting two guards who were so far away it would have been almost impossible to hit them with anything but a rifle, but he did. Both guards went down like two sacks of...

We moved forward together, the five of us—me, Franco, the two soldiers from the back of the truck, and the young soldier who'd been sitting next to me. We covered each other as we ran to the other vehicles that had entered the rear gate and were now parked in a circle in the middle of the courtyard. Two of the trucks had mounted guns and were firing short bursts at anything that moved. The noise was earsplitting.

As we ran, one of the soldiers from our truck took two hits in the back. He was wearing a vest, but the impact knocked him down, yelling in pain. Because he wasn't moving, he became an easy target and, as I turned my head to look back at him, I saw him get hit three more times; two in the back and one in the head. And he lay still.

We ran on toward the circle of trucks. I saw TJ appear from behind one of the Jeeps. He dropped to one knee, raised his M4 and began firing single shots.

I was moving fast. I skidded to a halt behind the Jeep as if I was sliding into second base.

TJ backed up, under cover of the Jeep, and shouted, "You okay, Harry?"

I nodded.

"I have you both tagged," Tim shouted in my earpiece. "Bob, too, but he's with another group. Oh shit! Watch out. Three o'clock."

TJ and I spun around as a truck, large C's painted on its sides and a heavy gun mounted in the bed, accompanied by at least a dozen soldiers on foot, rolled out from behind a building away to the right. The soldiers opened fire. The bullets tore into our vehicles. Our soldiers returned fire. It seemed as if the world was exploding around me.

TJ grabbed the back of my vest and hauled me out of the line of fire. We moved to the left together, toward the front of the Jeep, then we both fired over the hood. I continued to fire until my magazine was empty. Hurriedly, I dropped the mag and replaced it. I saw three of our CDN soldiers go down. We were taking heavy casualties. We were in trouble.

Gunfire was coming at us from the main building as well as from the soldiers on foot on both sides of the truck.

"Tim," I yelled. "Can you see an opening anywhere?"

"Head towards the main building," Tim yelped. "You're about to get help."

Help? They're frickin' killing us!

But we did as Tim said. TJ and I slipped between the trucks. I cocked the M4 as a group of jail guards and Carbena thugs came out of the main building and moved toward us at a half-crouch, firing their weapons as they came.

But they didn't see what we did, for behind them, dozens of inmates, armed with iron pipes and what looked like lengths of two-by-four, came pouring out of the jail's back door.

The Carbena thugs had no warning until the first of them went down as a length of heavy pipe smashed into the back of his neck.

The thugs turned, tried to fight back against the inmates, but they were quickly overwhelmed.

Tacca-tacca-tacca. The mounted machine gun on the truck with the C's opened fire again, not on us, but on the inmates. The 50-cal' bullets tearing into them. Heads exploded. Limbs were torn off. The ground beneath their feet turned red with blood.

But the Carbenas had made a fatal mistake. Instead of keeping us pinned down, by shifting their focus they'd opened themselves up to attack, and Franco's men were quick to take advantage. The CDN soldiers, highly trained as they were, made every shot count and, within seconds, the courtyard was cleared and we were moving into the jail's main building.

We were in a vast empty room... empty except for

maybe forty or fifty trestle tables, and it was dark, lit only by a row of windows that stretched the entire length of the right side of the room. I figured we were in the prison dining room.

I saw Bob up ahead of us. He disappeared along a corridor, running, firing as he went.

Franco and a group moved off in another direction. I hesitated for a moment, trying to decide if I should stay with Franco or go after Bob. I hesitated just a second too long and... suddenly TJ and I were alone.

I looked at him and said, "What the hell do we do now?"

"I can guide you," Tim said. "Just follow my directions."

35

Thursday, July 24, 2019

Thirty minutes after dawn

Gunfire echoed up and down the dark corridors of the jail, lit only by small, incandescent light bulbs hanging from the ceiling every few yards.

TJ and I were joined by a couple of CDN soldiers and we moved quickly forward, following Tim's directions. The two CDN men followed us, keeping an eye on our rear and on us, I was sure.

"Keep going straight," Tim said. "Then make a right at the next junction."

We rounded the corner only to hear Tim shout, "Look out! Guards at the next corner."

I dropped to a crouch, my M4 at the ready. TJ dropped down beside me. The two CDN soldiers, without the benefit of comms, stumbled to a halt behind us, confused, but they followed suit.

As soon as the guards rounded the corner, we opened fire. Two of them fell before they could figure out what was happening. A third managed to get off a couple of shots before his knee exploded and he went down screaming and dragged himself back around the corner.

I scooted over, hugging the wall. Someone was yelling up ahead. I could hear gunfire coming closer, and then it stopped, and I was sure we were about to come under attack again.

The shouting started up again, growing louder. More gunfire. We hunkered down, weapons at the ready, aimed at the corner up ahead.

"It's okay, Harry," Tim said. "Move forward, to the corner."

And we did. We moved to the corner, and there in the corridor we saw Franco and his men. The corridor behind them was littered with dead guards.

Franco smiled at me and said, "You did well, Tennessee."

And it was at that moment when I saw him. Just behind Franco, his wrists bound in front of him with zip ties, stood Ricky "*El Coco*" Mendoza. His face was bruised and dirty. He was wearing a gray, western-style shirt, dirty and ripped at one shoulder.

"You!" he snarled at me. "What are you doing here, Harry Starke? You have aligned yourself with this snake?" He motioned with his chin toward Franco.

"I don't really care what happens between the two of you," I said. "I'm here for Henry Stern."

"Who?" El Coco smiled, blood on his teeth. "That man doesn't exist, Starke. You killed the Texas Ranger."

One of Franco's soldiers punched him in the mouth, hard. His head snapped back, then forward. He coughed, spit blood, which dripped onto his expensive crocodile skin boots, and shook his head.

"The game's over, Mendoza," I said. "The US authorities already know I was framed, and I'm going to get my hands on Stern one way or another."

We heard gunshots echoing from somewhere deep inside the jail.

"Harry?" Tim's voice came into my ear. "I'm putting Bob through."

"You need to get over here, Harry," Bob said. "Your twin's about to get away."

I nodded to Franco. "I'll be back. I have a fish to catch."

Franco nodded back. "Go on, Tennessee. We still have to get this place locked down." Then he nodded at the two CDN soldiers who'd been following and said, "Go with them. See that nothing bad happens to them." He said it in English, a warning to us, no doubt.

"Lead me to them, Tim," I said, motioning for TJ to follow me.

And we ran.

As we ran, we saw inmates everywhere, bloody and smiling, some of them dragging the bodies of Carbena thugs behind them. The thugs looked as if they'd been beaten to death.

As we ran past one group of inmates, they saluted us and one of them yelled, "*Viva Nuevo Laredo.*"

I glanced at TJ and said, "What is this?"

TJ grinned. "It's the peaceful transition of power, my friend."

"Stop," Tim said in my ear. "There are three guards coming your way. They don't seem to be armed though."

The three guards came around the corner, two of them holding the third up between them. He had a gunshot wound to the shoulder. They were unarmed and looked scared.

They stopped dead when they saw us.

"*Por favor*," one of them pleaded.

TJ raised his rifle.

"No," I yelled, slapping the barrel down before he could pull the trigger.

I pushed the three guards against the wall.

"What do you want to do with them, then?" TJ asked.

"*Por favor*," the man repeated. Then he said something else I couldn't understand.

I looked around, spotted an open door, stepped away and looked inside. It was small, empty, with a single iron bed frame inside and a heavy bolt on the outside of the door. I motioned them inside, slammed the door shut behind them and slid the bolt across locking them inside.

"When they're found, they'll just kill them anyway," TJ said.

"Yes, maybe," I said. "But not us. That's not who we are, TJ."

TJ shrugged and followed me as we moved on, following Tim's directions.

We could hear more gunfire up ahead.

"What's happening, Tim?" I asked.

"It's Bob and some of Franco's men," he replied. "They have a bunch of Carbenas pinned down who are trying to escape."

"Escape? Is there another exit, then?" I craned my neck around the corner, trying to see what was happening. I pulled back as gunfire erupted again and bullets ricocheted off the walls. All I saw was a staircase that led down into darkness.

"There's a tunnel down there," Bob shouted.

I heard him both in person and through the comms.

"Some have already gotten away."

Oh hell, not Henry Stern!

I waited for a lull in the gunfire, then we, the four of us, ran forward and joined Bob and his now very small group of two CDN soldiers, and we took turns laying down cover fire.

TJ jumped forward, inching his way toward the stairs. He took cover in an open doorway and laid down cover for me and Bob. The CDN soldiers followed our lead and moved forward with us. They hadn't gone more than a couple of yards when one of them took a bullet to the throat and collapsed, coughing blood.

By the time we reached the staircase, there were only two Carbenas left alive, and they gave up. They dropped their weapons and stuck their hands in the air. Dead bodies littered the staircase.

The CDN soldiers quickly tied their hands and Bob, TJ and I ran down the stairs.

"How many have gotten away, Tim?"

"Not many. A few. It looks like several more are

about to go in. The stairs curve and the tunnel is just to the right. *Watch out!*" he yelled. "Two of them have turned around. They know you're coming."

I jumped to the left and then tumbled down the last few steps, bullets flying over my head, my M4 clattering on the steps behind me. I ended up in a heap at the bottom of the stairs and lay still, hoping the Carbena thugs at the entrance of the tunnel would think I'd been hit. They didn't.

One of them raised a handgun, pointing it in my direction. I rolled to my right, grasping at the CZ under my left arm. I pulled it and fired as I rolled, shot after shot after shot.

I didn't hit a damn thing, but I sure as hell made them move.

I ended up in a corner just as the last man—at least I thought he was the last man—turned and crawled inside a hole barely big enough for someone to crouch in.

A second later I saw four more men standing together, off to one side, seemingly frozen. Only one of them was armed and, as I swung my weapon toward him, he threw his weapon down.

Now you may be thinking I was all on my own down there. I wasn't. Bob was right behind me, yelling in Spanish, covering them as they dropped to their knees.

I looked at the four men, their hands linked behind their heads, hoping to spot my lookalike, but all of them were Mexican. Henry Stern wasn't among them.

I did recognize one face, though: the devilish, angular face with the dark eyes and the sharp, little goatee. The man who'd been in charge when I was brought across the river.

I stood up, stepped up to him and stuck the muzzle of my CZ under his chin.

"Bob," I said, without taking my eyes off Goatee's, "ask him where Henry Stern is."

Bob translated.

Goatee just smiled.

The floor shook as something somewhere exploded.

I jerked back, startled, and Goatee jumped forward, grabbing my weapon with both hands.

Before I could even move, TJ jumped forward, rammed the barrel of his M4 into Goatee's chest and pulled the trigger.

Goatee let go of my gun and staggered back, blood pouring from the wound. He backed slowly to the concrete wall, his hands covering the wound, then slid slowly down to the floor. That devilish smile never left his face, even as the life in his eyes flickered and died.

Smoke and dust billowed out of the tunnel entrance.

Bob, TJ and I looked at each other.

"They've blown the tunnel," TJ said. "What the hell do we do now?"

"So we can't follow them," I muttered. Then I cursed under my breath.

Has he gotten away? I wondered. *Or is his body buried under a thousand tons of dirt inside the tunnel?*

"Harry?" Tim said in my ear. "Four guys got out of the tunnel. We can see them clearly now that we don't need infra-red. One of them is a white guy."

"Stern," I yelled. "We have to move." And I turned to

run up the stairs, just as Franco and his men came down them. He had one of the .44s in his hand and he was smiling.

"We have succeeded, Tennessee," he said. "The jail is secure. The Carbenas in the fortress have surrendered. Most of the fighting is over."

"That's good," I said. "But my man is still at large. I have to go get him before he disappears." And I took a step forward.

But Franco raised the .44 and pointed it at me. The soldiers behind him also raised their weapons and pointed them at the three of us.

"Not so fast, my frien'," Franco said quietly. "There is still one more part of our deal for you to perform, remember? You are to be my hostages."

I had no option. I let my CZ fall to the floor and said, "Fine, Franco. If that's what we have to do."

"It is."

In a blur of motion, he swung the big revolver and slammed it into the side of my head.

36

Thursday, July 24, 2019

Early morning

The left side of my head exploded in fiery pain, from my cheekbone to the tip of my ear.

I staggered sideways, grunted in pain, then rubbed my face with my hand. The tips of my fingers came away bloody.

You son of a bitch. The foresight of that frickin' revolver split the top of my ear...

I straightened, stared at Franco, my hand to my bleeding ear, my eyes narrowed in hate, but I didn't retaliate. I couldn't. I'd have been shot dead in a second. Thankfully, neither Bob nor TJ made a move, either.

You'll pay for that, Franco. One day.

"There," Franco said, stepping close to inspect my face. "Now you really look like a Carbena prisoner. We do not have much time, *mi amigo*. If we had, I would take out a few of your teeth with pliers." He shrugged, then continued, "We will hope that the police do not look at you too closely."

"Let's hope, indeed," I muttered, the sarcasm dripping from my lips.

"Well then, let us go, Tennessee. Your friends will stay inside the complex, out of sight."

Franco turned and led the way up the stairs, through the maze of corridors until, finally, we came to an exit in a section of the jail I hadn't seen before.

Bob and TJ were held back while one of the soldiers put a zip tie around my wrists, just like El Coco had, and I grunted again as the guy pulled the tie way tighter than necessary.

We emerged at the main gate. There were guard towers on either side with a walkway between them. The towers were riddled with holes. Dead guards and Carbena thugs were being dragged away by CDN men and inmates. They waved and cheered Franco as we walked by, shouting at him in Spanish.

It was clear he was now their leader, and that the Carbena cartel in Nuevo Laredo was no more.

"Remember," Franco muttered as we reached the steps and began the climb up to the walkway, "if they ask you anything, you were kidnapped by Carbenas and brought here against your will. I've liberated you."

I glared at him.

"I remember. The Carbenas are bad and you're the hero. I got it."

Franco grinned. "You learn fast, Tennessee."

We climbed the steps. The jail wall was just about waist high to the walkway.

I looked out over the wall. Below I could see no less than a dozen blue and white trucks and as many cars, each with the logo *Policia Estatal de Tamaulipas* emblazoned along the sides and on the fronts. The soldiers and officers were all dressed in black—black vests, shirts, pants, helmets, and masks covering their faces.

All were armed with automatic rifles, and every one of them was aimed at me. At least that's what it felt like. In actuality, they were aimed at Franco, who was standing beside and behind me.

So, the hero of Nuevo Laredo isn't above using a human shield, huh?

Franco took a knife from his pocket, cut my hands free, pushed me forward, closer to the wall, and shouted something in Spanish.

A car door opened and a uniformed officer without a mask or helmet stepped out. His black hair was streaked with gray. He called something to Franco. Franco replied, nodding, and the conversation continued for several minutes, all in Spanish, so I had no idea what they were saying. At one point, Franco gently clapped me on the shoulder and said something about *El Americano* and *Los Carbenas*.

The officer took a long look at me, then at Franco. Then he looked again at me and said in heavily accented English.

"What this man is saying... is it true, sir?"

I shrugged and said, "I'm sorry, I don't speak Spanish. What did he say?"

"He say that you were kidnapped by the Carbenas? By El Coco?"

"Yes, I was. They captured me in Laredo and brought me across the river in a small boat."

The officer stared up at me for a long moment, then nodded and said, "You are lucky El Coco did not decide to have his fun with you."

"I was told he had plans to kill me slowly," I said. "I'm very glad he didn't get the chance."

There was a pause, so I decided to add, "And so are my friends in the United States. Very powerful friends."

The officer chuckled. "I watch American news, Mr. Starke. I know you have powerful friends. Mr. de la Cruz has promised to get you to Laredo. Do you trust him? We can escort you, if you wish."

Now that was an interesting proposition. No, I didn't completely trust Franco to keep his word. On the other hand, I didn't know if I could trust this guy and his motley crew of masked Policia either.

"Thank you, sir, but if Franco has said he'll take me to Laredo, I trust him to do so."

He'd frickin' better, after all the trouble I've gone through to help him.

Finally, the officer nodded and looked back at Franco, saying something in Spanish. I figured it must have meant: *You're in charge now. I'll expect my check the first of each month.*

Then the police officer climbed back into the truck and, seconds later, they all drove away, around the jail and... Who the hell knows where?

Meanwhile, in the dim, early morning light, the

clouds were gathering and a chill wind blew in from the north.

How fitting. A cold wind with the change of power.

Franco watched them go, then laughed and slapped me on the back. "*Fantastico* job, Tennessee. Did you notice how they did not try to enter the jail? They have no jurisdiction here. We have jurisdiction. The Cartel del Norte is in charge now."

I wasn't exactly in the mood to celebrate, so I said, "Franco, I'd love to stay and party with you, but I have a lookalike to track down and take back to Texas with me."

Franco pointed to the stairs and said, "Go, my friend. Your friends are waiting for you. I wish you much luck."

He turned to one of his lieutenants and nodded. The man handed me a CZ75.

"Take care of it," Franco said. "You will need it, I think."

I took the weapon and slipped it into the holster under my left arm, turned and started down the stairs.

"Oh, and Tennessee?" he said, an edge to his voice.

I stopped halfway down the steps and turned. "Yes?"

"Do not *ever* come back to Nuevo Laredo. If you do, I might have to kill you. Or not. I don't know. I will decide if it happens."

"Thanks for the warning, *mi amigo*."

Franco laughed at my sarcasm, and I turned and walked, a little unsteadily, down the stairs.

37

Thursday, July 24, 2019

Mid-morning

I stepped off the bottom step—which was surrounded by CDN soldiers all grinning and laughing together—and tapped my earpiece.

"Tim, are you there?"

"You bet, Harry."

"Please tell me you have eyes on Henry Stern."

"Yessir. Of course. We're on the road, less than a mile behind him. Jacque's driving and, so far, nobody's noticed the drone in the sky. And, before you ask, Nacho is with us. I've explained the gravity of the situation, and he's happy for us to go after him."

"Thanks, Tim."

As I began to run across the courtyard toward the rear gate where Bob and TJ were waiting for me, the first fat drop of rain hit my nose, followed immediately by another.

I sure as hell hope that military drone is weather resistant.

The CDN soldiers must have been told that we were free to go because no one tried to stop me or get in my way. And then I had a thought: we didn't have a vehicle.

I looked at Bob. He and TJ were just outside the gate. He had his phone at his ear and appeared to be yelling at someone.

The twins?

I ran on across the courtyard, past two long lines of bound Carbena thugs, all on their knees. They were surrounded by twenty, or so, CDN soldiers, all of them armed. One of who was issuing orders, I think.

I reached the gate just as Bob closed his phone. I looked at him and said, "What's that all about?"

Bob glanced back at the prisoners. "The CDN's giving them a chance to change loyalties. If not, they'll be shot."

"Most will switch, I bet," TJ said.

I tended to agree with him. Franco wasn't going to give them any other option.

A red Ford Explorer pulled up just outside the gate; Tony driving, Tito at his side.

The air was damp. The wind was picking up, refreshingly cold, and the raindrops continued to fall as we climbed into the rear seats.

A minute later, the SUV was rumbling back along the same dirt path we'd traveled to the jail not more than two hours earlier. It seemed like a lifetime ago.

The rain increased and hammered the windshield as we sped away from the jail and Franco de la Cruz, and I hoped to hell I'd never have the misfortune to set eyes on him again.

"Can you give us directions, Tim?" I said.

"I'm directing Tito, actually," Tim replied. "Hold on a sec. I'll put you all on the channel."

There was a click and Tim said, "Can you hear me now?"

Where have I heard that before? I thought, smiling to myself.

"Yes," I replied. "Loud and clear." Then to Tony, "Can we go any faster?"

Tony nodded and hit the gas. The SUV surged forward, speeding down one narrow street after another.

"Hold on," Tony yelled. Half a second later, we hit a speed bump, at full speed, and all four wheels left the ground and I literally came off my seat.

The tires squealed as we turned corners. I took the CZ75 from my shoulder holster. It wasn't a CZ Shadow like the one I'd purchased less than a month earlier, but it was better than my old VP9. I checked the load and placed it on my knee. Bob and TJ did the same.

Tony didn't slacken his speed, not even for a second. We'd gone no more than a couple of miles when we drove past an open cornfield. I noticed two thugs on a motorcycle speeding through the corn as if the devil was after them, and he was. The driver was bent low over the handlebars. The guy on the back was half twisted around, a gun in his hand.

Behind them were three more motorcycles, in a V

formation. In the lead, the Kid was riding hard, his machine leaping into the air as it hit one bump after another.

The rider on the back fired a series of shots at the Kid, but his shots went wild.

The Kid and another of the bikers raised their guns, firing. The thug on the back of the bike was hit, and so was the rear tire. The rear of the bike bounced high in the air and the thug who'd been shot cartwheeled off and disappeared into the corn. The bike was out of control, its rider trying to stay with it, but to no avail. The front wheel turned hard to the left and dug in. The bike somersaulted and the driver was thrown clear.

We turned a corner at the far end of the field, tires screaming, and I was able to see the Kid ride up to the thug that had been driving the bike. He was hurt and crawling along the dirt. The Kid put both feet on the ground, raised his weapon and fired two shots into the man's back.

"Peaceful exchange of power, my ass," Bob said.

How many Carbena thugs and—what did they call them? Halcones? *How many of them would be hunted down and killed over the next days and weeks?* It didn't bear thinking about.

Five minutes later we were on a four-lane highway, heading south, towards Monterrey.

Tony hit the gas hard. I watched as the needle hovered close to ninety as he weaved back and forth, dodging the slower traffic, and I hoped to hell we didn't run into any cops. If we were stopped for speeding...

Fortunately we weren't, and the Explorer drew inexorably closer to our prey.

The rain increased, hammering the windshield as the wipers fought to keep it clear. Lightning flashed in the clouds above. Visibility dropped almost to nothing as the windshield became a river and Tony was forced to slow down to seventy, sixty, fifty… as the storm raged around us.

If speeding on a highway in the rain was dangerous, Tony didn't seem to care. He opened his window, stuck his head out and hit the gas again. The road ahead had cleared as more sensible drivers pulled off to wait out the storm.

"Holy shit!" Bob said. "This is frickin' crazy."

"There's a military checkpoint ahead," Tim shouted. "But I don't think it's military. The vehicles are… They're Carbena and Henry's truck is heading right for them. He's maybe ten minutes away. I don't think you'll be able to catch him."

I cursed. "We can't let him get away. Not now. Anybody got any ideas?"

Tony yelled, "I know a back road we can take to try and beat Stern to Monterrey. Maybe we can find him there."

I frowned. "Among the millions that live in that city? It could take months, and we don't even know if he'll continue on to Monterrey or stay with the Carbenas."

TJ looked down at his pistol and said, "And we sure as hell don't have what we need to take the checkpoint."

"Harry?" It was Jacque. "I have an idea, but Franco might not like it."

"Franco already told me he'd kill me if he sets eyes on me again," I said, "so his feelings don't mean a whole hell of a lot, not right now."

"Okay, well, I was thinking..."

Jacque told us her idea.

Tim didn't like it. Neither did Nacho, but it brought a smile to TJ's face.

I looked at him, then at Bob. TJ nodded. Bob shrugged. I nodded back.

"Go for it," I said.

Dear God, I hope this works.

38

Thursday, July 24, 2019

Late Morning

The rain was bucketing down when we drove slowly by the van Nacho and Tim had turned into our mobile tech center. Jacque smiled and waved at us as we passed them.

About fifty yards ahead, a pickup truck was half in and half out of the ditch at the side of the road beside a broken telephone pole. Just beyond the wrecked truck, on the hard shoulder, lying there like a giant spider was the big black drone.

Tim had sent it flying into the truck's windshield.

Let's just hope to God that Stern didn't die in the crash.

As soon as the Explorer came to a stop and I jumped

out, my question was answered as gunfire exploded from behind the truck.

I dropped to a crouch and returned fire. Bob and one of the twins ran off to one side, wading through the tall grass to flank the thugs.

TJ joined me and we moved in the opposite direction.

As we neared the truck, a figure sprang up from behind a bush, gun raised. TJ and I fired in unison. The guy went down with a groan without firing a shot.

We approached cautiously. The man was Mexican. Not Henry Stern.

I ran to the truck and got there at the same time as Bob and Tony, and just in time to see Henry Stern crawl out through the shattered rear window.

He grunted as he fell out, tumbling into the mud and rushing rainwater. He staggered to his feet, turned to run, saw us and reached for a gun.

"Don't!" I shouted.

Henry froze.

I needn't have bothered. The holster at his hip was empty.

Finally, realizing he was finished, Stern raised his hands.

I stepped forward and said, "Henry Stern... My, my. You've been a bad, bad boy."

Bob snickered.

Even in the rain, it looked like Henry's face was turning red. "This doesn't mean a thing, Starke. Kill me if you want. You're a wanted man. Always will be."

I smiled and shook my head. "Oh, Henry, I'm not

going to kill you. I'm taking you back with me. You're going to stand trial for the murder of Cory Sloan, Texas Ranger."

"Hah. You think it's that easy? I happen to have a rock-solid alibi for the night Sloan was killed. And don't forget, your prints are on your gun. Not mine."

I reached forward, grabbed him by the shoulder, and hauled him out of the ditch. He didn't bother to resist.

"I hope your alibi's better than your framing job, Henry boy," I said as we climbed back up to the highway. "Because my lawyer has already filled that one full of holes big enough to fly a 747 through. How much you want to bet that your alibi's already fallen to pieces?"

He didn't answer.

We heard knocking from inside the crashed truck. We all turned to see two men trapped inside, in the front seats.

One of them yelled something in Spanish.

"They want us to let them out," Bob said. "What do you think?"

I shrugged, then said, "Why don't we just let Nacho give Franco their position and let him decide what to do with them. I'm done with this cartel war."

When we arrived back at the van and the SUV, Jacque was out on the pavement, smiling.

She looked at Henry and then back to me, shaking her head. "Wow, Harry. He's the spitting image of you."

"I know," I said. "I just wish he'd decided to be a PI instead of a dirtbag. Just think of the money we could make if there were two of me."

"Hah!" Henry Stern scoffed.

I slapped him upside the back of his head. "Hey, buddy, you don't get a say. You murdered a cop in cold blood. You're going down, my friend."

"Hah," Stern repeated. "We'll see about that."

Bob stepped forward, grabbed him roughly by the collar, shoved him toward the Explorer and forced him to climb in.

"Yeah, buddy," Bob growled. "We sure will. Now get in and buckle up."

I turned to Jacque and said, "Thanks, Jacque. Whatever would I do without you?"

Jacque grinned. "It was actually kind of fun. I felt like I was in a spy movie."

"Well, let's get back to town and get cleaned up."

"Sure thing, Harry. I know the way. I memorized it, remember?"

39

Thursday, July 24, 2019

Afternoon

The storm raged on for more than an hour before the rain finally tapered off.

By that time, we'd arrived downtown and found a small motel just a few blocks from the US-Mexico border and paid for a room. We stayed just long enough to shower and change clothes. Jacque, bless her, had clean underwear, jeans and tees for all, except for the twins and Henry Stern. Nacho and Tim said their good-byes. Nacho, much to Tim's embarrassment, hugged him, muttered something in Spanish, then climbed into the van and drove away.

The hotel was old and dingy, but the water was hot and the AC was cold. I took my time in the shower, washing away the days of sweat and grime.

I stepped out into the bright, sunny hot street. But the heat didn't bother me anymore. We had my lookalike and were going home.

Across the street was a plaza, the same plaza Bob and I had visited the other day to talk to the man named Jose.

Bob and Tito were sitting on one of the park benches. Between them sat a very unhappy, and very dirty, Henry Stern. His shoes and jeans were caked with mud. I smiled as I walked across the road to join them. I had no sympathy for him; not one bit.

TJ, Jacque, and Tim joined us a couple of minutes later, each with a cup of flavored shaved ice covered with brightly colored fruit syrup.

"Okay, guys," I said as I handed Jacque my room key. "You will stay here until the coast is clear. I'll have August call you when it's okay for you to go across."

"Right," Jacque said. "When you're sure they won't arrest us, you mean."

I nodded. "Grab some lunch, and if you have to stay the night, just get a second room. Charge it on the company card."

Jacque waved me off. "I can handle it, Harry."

"Oh, I know you can. All of you." I suddenly felt a lump in my throat and I paused, looked down at my brand new knockoff Nike shoes for a moment, then looked up and said, "Thank you. All of you."

I looked at each of them in turn. Jacque, Tim, TJ, Bob, and finally each of the twins.

Tito gave me a little salute. "We're heading off now, *mi amigo*. But if ever you need help, Bob knows how to find us."

"Thanks..." I said.

I would have said more, but they'd already turned away. They walked across the street and disappeared into the crowds.

I took a deep breath, looked at Bob and said, "You ready to do this?"

"You got it, boss."

We escorted Henry Stern through downtown Nuevo Laredo to the border, to what the map called Bridge One.

We paid five pesos each to access the bridge and began the walk across. I looked down at the Rio Grande flowing peacefully under the bridge, and I smiled. *Not long now.*

There was a line at the US end of the bridge, but we bypassed it. We figured the border patrol wouldn't mind, since they'd be happy to arrest us both: me and Henry Stern.

At least that's what I hoped.

Bob spoke quietly with an officer near the entrance to the Customs offices and flashed a badge and an ID.

I wonder what that is? CIA Spook?

Whatever it was, the officer nodded and turned toward Stern and me, a hand on his gun.

He looked at each of us, back and forth, several times, then said, "Uh, which is Harry Starke?"

I squeezed Henry's arm and said, "I am."

"Okay," the officer responded. "I'm taking both of you in for questioning."

Henry's face turned red. "Not me, surely. I'm not wanted. I'm a law-abiding US citizen."

The officer frowned at him. "It's called national security, sir. I don't need a warrant to detain you."

I looked at Henry and smiled. "We'll both be happy to be detained for questioning, won't we, Henry? After all, you have nothing to hide, right?"

He pursed his lips, looked at me and said, "I'm going to kill you, Starke. One of these days. You just mark my words."

"Oh dear, Henry. I've heard that somewhere before... Now who was it? Oh yeah. I remember. Think again, dummy."

I turned to the officer. "We're all yours, sir."

Behind him, Bob waved at me as he slipped into the Customs office and out of sight.

Godspeed, Bob. Until we meet again.

40

Thursday, July 24, 2019

Late afternoon

I was put into a small room with a stainless steel table. Border patrol officers came and went. Some asked me questions. I told my story—well, an abbreviated version of it—at least a dozen times. And the hours passed.

Whenever I tried to ask any questions of my own, I was met with either stony silence or a firm "no."

No, I couldn't use the phone.

No, I couldn't call my wife.

No, I couldn't call my lawyer.

No, I couldn't be told where Henry Stern was.

It went on so long that, eventually, I began to get worried that everything we'd done over the past week had been for nothing. If they'd let Stern go, I'd probably never find him again. And even if Raymundo and my father succeeded in getting me off the hook for the murders, justice would never truly be served.

Finally, after what felt like an eternity, two Laredo police officers arrived with orders to transport me to the local police department.

The two officers were just as unhelpful as the border patrol. As they walked me out to the squad car, they refused to answer a single question. In fact, they refused to speak to me at all.

I was taken to the same cage I'd been in before. The mood in Laredo's police department was... abysmal. And who could blame them? They'd lost two of their own, and that less than a week after a well-loved, local Texas Ranger had been gunned down in cold blood.

The two law enforcement officers had been killed in the line of duty. They had no idea they were just pawns in Shady's deadly game. I felt sorry for them, and for all their friends on the force that had to deal with their loss.

I was given absolutely zero information. I was about to start raising a stink about not getting to see my lawyer when the door at the end of the room opened, and in walked—I should say shuffled—Henry Stern, shackled and handcuffed and led by three officers who placed him in the cage next to mine.

Stern was not at all happy. He glared at me, his face red.

I smiled at him, feeling like a kid that had just been told he was going to McDonald's to get a Happy Meal and an ice cream.

"Well, well, well," I said to Stern. "It looks like you couldn't talk your way out of it, huh?"

Stern didn't speak. He sat down, hard, on his bunk and stared up at the ceiling.

Me? I lay back on my own bunk, smiling, knowing that whatever came next, I'd gotten Stern for the murder. And that my team would be able to prove it.

I t was about an hour later when the door opened again, and in walked my old friend from my first visit, Lieutenant Stanley Door. He nodded and smiled at me. Behind him was Raymundo, my new lawyer from Austin, along with August, and Amanda, holding Jade.

"You're getting out of here, Mr. Starke," Door said as he opened my cage door.

"I made bail?"

"Bail? Hah. The DA's dropped all charges against you, for Sloan's murder, and for the other murders you were charged with. You're free to go, and good luck to you, sir."

I strode out of the cell, wrapped my arms around Amanda, kissed her. Then I turned her loose and took Jade from her, held her gently in my arms and kissed her forehead. She looked as if she'd just woken up from a nap, and she gazed up at me with those magical, green eyes.

August patted me on the back and said, "Well done, son."

Stanley Door turned to Stern. "You, sir, however, have a lot of explaining to do."

Stern stepped to the bars, grabbed them with both hands and said, "You can't hold me in here. I haven't been arrested."

"Well now, don't you worry about that," Door said amiably. "The boys upstairs are typing up the warrant for you, special, like. We'll make your stay with us official. Then I will be legally obligated to provide you with a shower and some dinner. Sound good?"

Stern didn't answer. He gripped the bars so tightly his knuckles turned white.

"I told you, Stern," I said. "You're going down, for a long time, unless... Well, unless they decide to give you the needle, which wouldn't surprise me, considering what you did to that Texas Ranger. That's a capital crime, you know."

Henry stared at me and practically growled like a rabid dog.

"Oh, my," Amanda said. "I knew he looked like you, but I didn't realize how much."

"I know," I said. "He's a handsome son of a gun, though, isn't he? That won't get him out of prison though."

Stanley Door laughed. "No, it won't. And Franco de la Cruz made sure of that."

I frowned. "What do you mean?"

They all looked at me.

"You don't know?" August said.

"No. I don't know... What?"

Raymundo took out his phone and pulled up a video.

"It's all over Facebook, *señor*. They'll probably show it on the local news tonight."

Ricky *"El Coco"* Mendoza was sitting on a metal folding chair facing the camera. His face was bruised and bloody. He'd obviously undergone some "special treatment."

El Coco began to speak, in Spanish, slowly and angrily. Subtitles showed along the bottom of the screen.

"I admit I framed Mr. Harry Starke for the murder of the Texas Ranger named Sloan. This I did as a favor for a Mr. Lester Tree, now dead. The real killer's name is Henry Stern. More details will be sent to the police and media shortly."

And then came the credit: "Translation and Subtitles courtesy of Ignacio 'Nacho' Reyes. Gracias."

I couldn't help but chuckle. Franco really had come through for me after all. After seeing that video, I was willing to forgive him just about anything, even the split ear.

Henry Stern had also been listening to the video. His shoulders slumped. He released the bars, turned, and went to his bunk and dropped down on it. And I had no doubt the words "capital punishment" were playing in his head.

"Well," I said to my wife, my father and my lawyer, "what are we waiting for? If I'm free to go, let's go get some dinner. My treat."

And we did.

41

Thursday, July 24, 2019

Evening

That evening we all ate at a Roadhouse Steakhouse. The Laredo PD had asked me to stick around for a short while so that I could sign an affidavit as to my earlier statement to the border patrol, and I was happy to do so. After dinner, Kate, Rose, Amanda, Maria and Jade went to take a nap and wait while I paid one last visit to the police department.

The two Texas Rangers—David Culp and John Booth—were there, and damned if they didn't apologize to me—even Booth—for dragging me from Tennessee to Laredo when I was actually innocent. I smiled and told them they had nothing to apologize for, that they were just doing their jobs.

And then Raymundo took me to one side and said I

should consider opening an Austin office, and that he alone would be able to keep us busy. I told him I'd think about it.

August had called Jacque, and she, Tim and TJ had crossed the border back into Texas without incident. By ten o'clock that evening, we were all aboard August's Gulfstream flying home to Tennessee.

When we landed, I told everyone to go home and take the next couple of days off. I knew we'd all been gone for far too long, and that the rest of my extended team had been sitting at home waiting for us to return, but work? No, I couldn't face it, not then. I needed to clear my head.

I took Kate to one side, held her close for just a minute and thanked her. I knew everyone was watching, including Amanda, but I didn't care. Friends like Kate come around but once in a lifetime, and I was infinitely grateful to her. I always would be, and I wanted her to know it.

42

Friday, July 28

Morning

I rose early that next morning, Wednesday, and swam several laps before heading out for a run. I needed to get back into shape. I felt like a badly tied bag of trash, and Bob's awful words "dad bod" still rang in my head.

By the time I got back to the house, just in time to make coffee for Amanda and change Jade's diaper, I had several messages from Jacque asking me to call her, so I did.

"Hey, Harry, I have a property I just have to show you."

"Does it have to be today, Jacque?" I said. "I really wanted to just relax with my family."

"Harry. Come on. I'm starting to think that you're

intentionally putting off setting up a new office."

"What? That's crazy." But even as I said the words, I had a deep-seated feeling that perhaps Jacque was right. I really loved my old office. Kate and I were an item when I'd first moved into it. She'd helped me design my inner sanctum, my perfect private office. Truth be told, I couldn't imagine any place being as good as that one. Call me sentimental if you want, but that's how I felt.

"Fine, Jacque. I'll look at one place only, so make it a good one."

"What I want to show you, Harry, isn't just good. It's perfect, I swear. I'll text you the address. Be there in thirty minutes?"

"Make it an hour. I promised to make Amanda breakfast."

"Okay. It's a deal."

The offices were part of a newly developed industrial complex by the river, less than a ten-minute drive from downtown, and it was upscale, right on the river and no doubt expensive.

I could get used to that.

Jacque was already there, waiting for me.

"Let me show you around," she said.

The ground floor was still unfinished. Only a few of the walls had been studded in, and none had been sheetrocked.

"This is good," Jacque said by way of explanation. "We can choose our own floor plan. I'm thinking a security room and a walk-in weapons locker on this floor. We can have the outer wall reinforced. What d'you think?"

I nodded as I thought of what had happened to my

old offices after the bomb blast. Yes, I could understand what she was thinking.

She pointed to one side of the building. "We could put the server room over there and Tim's office right next to it. Plus, we'd have room for a full technical team. Two or three additional people, maybe."

She motioned with her hand. "The reception area would be here. A public conference room here," she said as she walked around the seemingly vast open space. "The break room could be over here and bathrooms, complete with showers, right here. You could even install a small gym, if you want to."

She looked at me, raising her eyebrows. I nodded.

"Now, follow me," she said as she started up the stairs.

The upper floor was just as open as the floor below. Jacque walked through the middle, turned to face me, raised her arms and twirled around. "My office, a second private conference room and... finally," she said and pointed to the corner with both hands. "Your new inner sanctum. A huge corner office with these floor-to-ceiling windows and an amazing view of the Tennessee River. Isn't it awesome?"

It was, and it reminded me of the view from the condo where I'd lived for years before I married Amanda. The view of the river, the lights on the Thrasher Bridge at night, they were... mesmerizing. The view from my new office would be even more spectacular.

"Jacque. This... this is—"

"If you don't like it," she said coyly, "I have a few other places we can look at."

"Jacque, you didn't let me finish," I said. "It's perfect."

I looked at her and smiled.

She was beaming. "I hoped you'd say that. There's room to grow here. And the industrial park will be all very upscale when it's finished. Oh, and we can get a permit for a helipad on the roof, too."

I laughed. "A helipad. Why would I want to land a chopper on the roof, Jacque?"

She shrugged. "I just thought you'd want to know. It's an option... And Tim will want a bigger drone now, after playing with that monster in Nuevo Laredo."

"I'm sure he will."

I looked around one last time, then walked over to the corner windows and stared out over the river I loved so much, and I nodded. It was breathtaking. *My new inner sanctum. I can see it already.*

"Do it, Jacque. Don't worry about the money. This is the new home of Harry Starke Investigations."

Jacque took out her phone and tapped in a short message. "I'll have to sign right away. You can sign later. I also have an interior architect out of Nashville I like. If it's okay with you, I'll have her draw up the plans and have something for you to look at by the end of the week."

I watched her work. This was Jacque at her best, in control, organizing and scheduling. She kept my business running smoothly. Making her my partner was the best business decision I'd ever made.

A helipad? A chopper on the roof? Could come in handy, I guess... Nah!

I couldn't wait to show Amanda.

EPILOGUE

Monday, July 26

Morning

Three days after Harry Starke arrived back in Chattanooga, Bob Ryan strode into the main lobby of a downtown office building in Dallas, Texas. He was smartly dressed in a dark gray business suit, white shirt, a royal blue tie and black Italian loafers.

The lobby was busy, people rushing this way and that, but he took no notice. He walked quickly to the security checkpoint located just in front of the bank of elevators and presented his ID.

The guard nodded, stepped around the desk and waved a wand over him. He found nothing other than a watch and belt buckle.

The guard nodded and waved him through. Bob nodded his thanks and stepped over to the elevators. He waited for an empty one, stepped in and pressed the button for the top floor.

The screen above the bank of buttons flashed and requested a security card. Bob took one from his wallet and presented it to the scanner. An image of an open padlock appeared on the screen and the elevator began to rise. The elevator rose quickly. Bob reached into his jacket and took a small .22 semi-automatic handgun from the holster under his left arm. The gun, and its integral silencer, were ceramic, undetectable by the electromagnetic security wand.

The elevator slowed to a stop, causing Bob's ear to pop. He took a deep breath. The door opened and he was greeted by two men wearing black suits.

Both men were taken by surprise as Bob snapped off two quick shots. They went down without a sound, each with a bullet in the center of his forehead.

The woman at the reception desk let out a yelp.

"Put your hands behind your back," Bob said. "Keep your mouth shut and I won't hurt you."

She did as she was told, and he tied her wrists with a plastic zip tie, then taped her mouth.

"Now sit still and be a good girl."

He turned and walked quickly along the hallway to a pair of double doors, pushed them open, stepped inside and was immediately surprised by another man in black.

The man saw the gun in Bob's hand and reacted instantly. He kicked the weapon from Bob's hand and clipped him with a punch to the jaw. Bob blocked a second punch, spun, swept the man's feet from under him with a roundhouse kick and reached for the carbon fiber knife on his belt. It, too, was undetectable by the magnetic wand.

By the time Bob had the knife in his hand, the man in black had leaped to his feet and was moving toward him. Bob sliced at him, forcing him to jump back. Bob stepped forward, stabbed at the man. The man sidestepped, grabbed Bob's arm with one hand then the other, and they both staggered across the room, Bob's superior strength slowly overcoming the smaller man. The knife-point was at the man's throat when...

"*Stop!*"

Bob eased up on the pressure, looked around, then stepped away. He'd been so surprised by the man in black that he hadn't noticed the huge desk at the far side of the room.

The woman was seated in a luxurious leather office chair, her back to him, looking out of the wall of windows over the Dallas skyline. "What are you doing here, Mr. Ryan?"

Bob stepped away from the man in black, walked to the desk, and slipped the carbon fiber knife back into its holster.

"I'm not here to kill you," he said.

She didn't turn around. "You didn't answer my question, Mr. Ryan. What are you doing here?"

"I need your help. I'm looking for a man. He took something from me... a long time ago. His name is Adam Spelhaus. And I think you know where he is. If not, I'm sure you know how to find him. So I'm asking for your help."

"My help? And what do I get in return?"

Bob sat down in front of the desk and said, "In return, I offer my services, no charge."

The woman laughed. "Hmm. Maybe there is something you can do for me, Mr. Ryan. But it could be... messy."

Bob shrugged. "Isn't it always when you're involved?" he said, half joking.

"I suppose it is." The woman turned slowly around and faced him. And Bob saw a face he hadn't laid eyes on in many years, a face that once had spurred a web of international intrigue, a face that once was displayed on every most wanted poster in every major country in the world.

The woman smiled at him. She was stunningly beautiful, as beautiful as she was deadly.

Her jet-black hair hung to her shoulders, and her soft, Asian features were the color of alabaster. She was wearing a black dress that clung to the contours of her body.

The woman in the chair had many names, but the name Bob knew her by was the one that struck terror in the hearts of men on every continent on the planet.

That name was... Cassandra Wu.

The End

ONE MORE THING

Thank you.

Thank you for reading *End Game*, the 16th novel in the Harry Starke series. I hope you enjoyed it. If you did, please consider telling your friends or posting a short review on Amazon (just a sentence will do). Word of mouth is an author's best friend and much appreciated. Thank you.

Blair Howard.

If you have comments or questions, you can contact me by email at blair@blairhoward.com, and you can visit my website http://www.blairhoward.com.

Join my mailing list and I'll give you the first book in the Harry Starke Series as a gift. For instant access just click this link and tell me where to send it:

http://dl.bookfunnel.com/j6ztln4ohc.

Made in the USA
Monee, IL
04 October 2022